Unravelling

KAREN HONNOR

DEDICATION

This is dedicated to Mary and Derek and to all the memories of family that have danced around my head when writing this.

ACKNOWLEDGMENTS

First and foremost to my family – Stuart, Matthew and Zoe. For my inspiration, my support to keep writing on the days when the task seemed too difficult to complete and for believing that I could do it. In particular, to Zoe for kick starting this project and helping me to organise my thoughts and to 'just write' without worrying about where it may or may not lead.

To Mum and Dad: Mary and Derek, for the stories of people and places and the moments in time that formed the background to my growing up. Though we lost Dad years ago, his presence continues to be felt through the memories we cherish and by that token, nobody is truly lost forever.

To Mary, Sheila, Pam, Irene and Jenny – the 'Monday Girls' for being collaborators in sowing the seeds that grew into the scenes and characters and moments of family life within these pages.

To Sara-Jane – friend, motivating force, sounding board and 'editor.' Thank you for believing in my writing from the outset.

To Sara – an inspiring creative writing tutor, for your encouragement and kind words, giving me the self-belief to give fiction writing a go.

To my 'story writing' consulting team – Zoe, Sara-Jane, Mary, Ruth and Jacqueline. Always ready to offer support, suggestions and a helping hand.

To the many friends, both actual and virtual, who have continued to support my writing in so many different ways, often the smallest gestures can have the most profound effect.

To all who continue to strive to find a cure for dementia and those who support and care for those affected by this disease. Remember the person you always loved is still there. This story is offered in celebration of the lives that they all have lived.

To Melissa Hawkes for the cover design.

INTRODUCTION

I lost my Dad twice.

That is the nature of dementia. He passed away in 2012 but that was the second loss, for we had all lost the man that he we knew him to be, several years earlier. Stroke and vascular dementia wore that person away. He too, of course, slowly lost himself.

In writing this story, I have wondered what that process must have been like. At the time, I could observe regular indicators of his frustrations and interpret the meaning of his conversations, according to my own understanding of them. But that would never equate to the sum total of his experiences, his perspective over the last years, and he could not express that to me.

At the time of writing this, it is predicted that 209,600 people in the United Kingdom will develop dementia this year. One every three minutes. That is a startling statistic. According to the Alzheimer's Society, this figure is projected to rise to 1.6 million people by 2040 which is a vast figure to comprehend.

When we are confronted with such facts and figures, I find there is a tendency to glaze over, to lose the details. Of course the detail reveals each of these figures as a person - an individual, a personality, a character within their own life experience. For each of these individuals, there will be a number of people associated with them who will also feel the effects, like the ripple effect upon a pond when a pebble is cast into it. Many lives touched and altered as a result.

The story written here is fictional. It does not tell the facts of one of these individuals but it aims to reflect a little of the journey that each of them may make. It is coloured by my experiences of watching a close relative struggle with the condition and in recognition of his immense strength of character.

I hope he would approve of the story I have told.

UNRAVELLING

1 JUST THE TICKET

Lucy brushed a tear from her cheek and allowed her gaze to focus through the blur onto the well-thumbed slice of the past that she was holding. Just a simple bus ticket. Insignificant at first glance and easy to discard as so many of its kind would have been in days gone by. Casually thrown away at the end of a mundane journey but this one was different, well it was to Doris.

A half-grin formed as Lucy recalled the day she had retrieved this. The vultures had already picked over the china and trinkets but you cannot put a price on all that is precious. Crouched in a corner of her Gran's dusty attic, Lucy had discovered the tin of random oddments, protected all these years by nostalgia and sentiment. It would have been so easy for this to have been scooped up with all the other scattered memories due to be cast aside during the house clearance. But Lucy sensed its significance.

Most people had stopped listening to Doris once she had been confined to the nursing home as her conversation lost its thread and her thoughts fox-trotted around. Not Lucy. She loved her Gran's stories and amongst their confused dance there was the sparkle of an odd gem of truth. At those moments the gentle pools of her gran's greying, blue eyes invited Lucy in. Just as a spool of old movie footage reveals a scene clicking frame by frame, she caught glimpses of the girl her gran used to be. Doris in her dancing days, in whirling petticoats with tumbling sandy brown locks catching the light as her feet marked the beat.

The rush of young love with a gaze exchanged across the dance floor may have become a faded memory for Doris but the tale of how they met, dodged the raindrops and held hands to take the bus ride home together, was her favourite to recall. In her rocking chair, crocheted blanket upon her knee and Lucy's wondrous 'treasure box find' placed beside a tray of tea, Doris was now content. The broken connections of life's confusion that usually frustrated Doris were strangely calm this afternoon. Lucy saw this peace reflected in the window pane's rivulets of rain.

With a determined effort Doris pressed the ticket into Lucy's palm, clasped her hand tight and returned her focus to the rain.

"Goodnight, sweetheart…"

A YEAR EARLIER

(2015)

2 GREEN MEADOWS

"Cantankerous and draining."

Those were the words she heard them using nowadays. In her prime there would have been terms of warmth, praising her looks and sociable nature - how her eyes twinkled as she tossed back her head to laugh in a crowded room, knowing full well that she had the attention of everyone there. Now there was little of that paid to Doris and although it may seem that she cannot follow the thread of what is going on around her, she still hears the whispers and exasperations.

When Doris calls for help for the eighth time that day, she hears the muttering under the breath and another part of her slowly dims. All this stuff of the nursing home, these silly rules and routines – they make no sense to her. A phrase floats into her head

"When I grow up, I'm going to break the rules and be free."

Doris closes her eyes and allows the phrase to carry her back to a warm summer and a grassy riverbank. There is a persistent wasp now caught within a glass bottle as punishment for its interest in the picnic – the consequence of curiosity. Beyond the confines of the glass prison all is open and free and Doris remembers the blue sky moment.

It was a day when she played that childhood game with her sister, Lillian, taking turns to make cloud dragons and islands, fantastical shifting creatures and faraway places free of limits, as imagination has no rules to follow. There was nothing particular at the time to mark the scene as a memory to treasure but doesn't life just have a habit of doing that?

Doris sat up, taking a break from the cloudscape before them to nibble the last of the jam sandwiches and looked at the tinge of colour kissing Lillian's freckled cheeks. The picnic remains cast crumbs across the tartan blanket but there was little left from this rare treat to share with any opportunistic ant straying from the grass. Refuelled by squash and sunshine, Doris watched Lillian skip off to climb a nearby tree. Mother would have disapproved of such a boyish activity, but Lillian never followed the rules.

Before laying back on the blanket to survey the clouds again, Doris returned her gaze to the poor wasp slipping down the inside of the bottle and she tentatively placed the bottle on its side. Keeping a safe distance, she watched as it regained its strength to find its freedom on the summer breeze, flying off into the distant blue.

***

"Blue," she said out loud. "Yes, blue tablet now, after lunch."

That was the ritual each day. There was some sort of stew usually and vegetables that she had forgotten the names of, then a sponge pudding with custard on a good day, before the drugs trolley came round. It was probably Tuesday today, a fact that made Doris smile. The weekly timetable on her wall had a picture of a vibrant, young face looking back at her. She could not quite get the name from the tip of her tongue but this girl frequently came to sit with her, to share the tea tray and hobnob biscuits and to let her talk without rushing her on to the next part of the day. The girl always came to join Doris on a Tuesday afternoon.

Doris thought she should make an effort to look presentable if her guest was coming soon. She picked up her Mason Pearson hairbrush from the dressing table and tried her best to make the wisps of white hair fall into place around the face in the mirror. She was not good with faces anymore and recognised little in the hollowing heart-shaped one that sat before her. Though she knew each wrinkle mapped the life she'd had, Doris dotted them haphazardly with a little powder from her compact before trying unsuccessfully to twist the lid back into place. It took a lot of concentration now to make her fingers move the way she wanted. Arthritis had slowly won the battle there, especially on damp days. Sadness pervaded as her gaze fell onto her thin hands and she moved her fingers slowly up and down, mirroring a silent melody line that they used to play somewhere before. Somewhere where the spotlight shone and glasses clinked in camaraderie. Now she grasped the bar of her walking frame and manoeuvred awkwardly into the corridor and towards the garden room. "Off we go, girl."

It had taken Doris a while to settle into her new surroundings at Green Meadows – the name rather euphemistically given to the place where the elderly and infirm were put out to pasture. Though the place was clean and comfortable, it was now a shadow of its former self and somewhat like its residents, only had hints about it of its former glory. The fading shades of the swirling carpet dulled the slippered footsteps that now shuffled along its corridors. Dotted about the statutory signage were sepia toned framed snapshots of local scenes, the odd landscape or still life painting and the occasional wall lamp wearing its tasseled hat at a jaunty angle. The high ceilings and ornate cornicing had survived in places but not everywhere. Some rooms which would have once commanded a moment of respect for their design and presence had been brutally sectioned into more functional areas – an office corner, housing for medical and cleaning equipment, staff lockers alongside a basic kitchenette where hastily grabbed coffees or microwaved lunches were prepared when the rota allowed them the breathing space to do so.

Doris now knew her way from her room to the communal areas of Green Meadows, well she did most days. Along the corridor, past the few doors to other residents' rooms and into the small lift – she was a little too unsteady to use the stairs now. Some days she managed to eat lunch in the dining room, when her joints behaved themselves and her mind felt calm enough to manage the many distractions there. Today she had eaten in her room, from a swiveling bed tray, whilst looking out of her bedroom window at the cherry blossom branches. That was when she had remembered the need for her Tuesday ritual and why she now found herself in the garden room, plumping up a floral cushion before lowering herself into the armchair by the bay window.

A couple of her fellow residents dozed off their dinners from their armchairs but Doris was alert. From her vantage point, she knew she could see past the potted ferns to spot the smile and youthful bouncing walk of her visitor. She would wait here a while for her, for she was sure it was Tuesday.

3 SUGAR SKETCHES

With her connection missed, Lucy was now half running from the bus stop, knowing that her Gran would be waiting for her. She would like to have more time to visit her but she had a lot to juggle. With her studies, a part-time shop job and a mission at home to keep her head down, do her chores when asked and keep her opinions to herself, there was little other spare time to devote. The youngest of four and the only girl, she was used to being ignored. She no longer competed for attention and used her drawing and her books as friends. Perhaps that was why she looked forward to her Tuesday afternoons at Green Meadows. She knew it would be quiet there and Gran may not fully recognise who she was, but she was always happy to see her and to share a story over tea and biscuits.

As she avoided last night's leftover puddles, Lucy checked in her canvas shoulder bag for the essentials. As always, she had picked up a packet of her Gran's favourite wine gums from the station kiosk, moving her fingers past the packet she fumbled around to feel for the shape of her tin of pencils and her sketchbook. She was reluctant to leave the house without them as she never knew when she might get a moment to add to her random collection of drawings but particularly on a Tuesday, in the peace and quiet of the garden room, she had fallen into the habit of drawing. Sometimes she could take down a likeness of Doris in full flow, reliving a past story with her face animating the details. Sometimes, when Doris cat-napped, Lucy would turn her attentions to other parts of the room, the garden or its other residents. She did not know what she would ever do with all these drawings but she found she could not break the habit now.

Green Meadows was in a leafy part of town, where the roads were wider and the houses all had sweeping driveways, setting them back from the passing traffic. The gravel crunched under foot and a stray piece somehow found its way into Lucy's grey suede Chelsea boot. She tried to ignore it as she stepped up to press the entrance buzzer and gave her name. Already late, she could manage a little discomfort for a while longer but all the same she wondered how the offending piece had now lodged itself in her heel.

It was late March and the weather was playing its usual game of roulette. Accordingly, Lucy had dressed in layers and after her brisk walk from the bus stop was feeling the need to take off her jacket. Here and there, raindrops remained on the leaves and the sun's rays caught their reflections as Lucy looked at spring's splashes of colour. There was an unspoken promise at this time of the year, ready to catch your eye if you took a moment to look for it.

"She's in the garden room, Lucy."

"Thank-you, I'm a bit late today."

"Don't worry, dear."

Lucy smiled back at the receptionist as she signed the visitor book and made light work of the walk past the office, dining room and TV lounge. She nodded as she passed several residents and members of staff, eagerly agreed to the tray of tea offered on arrival and beamed at her Gran as she stretched out her hands to greet her.

"Time for a chat, Gran?" Lucy chirped.

"Oh yes, I think so. What's your name again, dearie?" Doris replied with a fleeting look of combined confusion and apology. "Never mind, names escape me," she continued, "I'm glad you're here."

Lucy had learnt not to let the lack of recall of her name upset her, for she knew that there was still a recognition deep within, a familiarity to their bond that stretched back to the times when she would climb onto her Gran's lap and ask for her to tell a bedtime story. After all, she was still doing that really as she sat down opposite Doris to let her chat her way through the afternoon. Today Lucy wondered what tales would unfold and she sat back in her chair and made ready to listen.

"Grab you coat and grab your hat…" Doris began singing and looked through the window. She tapped her fingers on the arm of her chair as she continued, "Dah, dah, dah, your feet, to the sunny side of the street."

Lucy smiled along to the tune, a familiar refrain from a different era, and poured out the tea as it arrived. She tried to imagine how the youthful version would have sounded and dropped two sugar cubes into her Gran's cup. This was the only place that Lucy knew where they served sugar cubes instead of those little paper packets. If no-one was looking, Lucy would usually sneak one out of the stainless steel bowl and pop it quickly into her mouth to suck upon until she had gathered her drawing resources out of her bag and arranged them on her lap. Today, she left the sugar and dunked a hobnob biscuit instead and made herself comfortable in her chair, sucking in the tea-soaked flavour as Doris spoke of sunshine and the blossom outside the window. Doris seemed to be in a good mood today, floating her thoughts along with the blossom petals on the spring breeze.

It was often like that with her Gran's thoughts and Lucy quite enjoyed seeing where each one would take them. She had grown to see it as a challenge, attempting to pin them down to their origin or on days like today, allowing them to take their own direction as a blend of half-facts and fantasy. There were names that Lucy recognised from previous tales today, featuring as little cameos among the more nonsensical phrases.

"And Lillian laughed – covered in mud she was!"

"Was she, Gran?"

"Yes, dear. Is she in her room?"

"I'm not sure."

"Got her nose in a book, I bet."

Most weeks, Lillian seemed to feature heavily and Doris kept asking when her younger sister would be coming to join them. Lucy usually managed to direct the conversation onwards so that the jumbled plot continued, sprinkled intermittently with lyrics from her youth.

Lucy took off her glasses and cleaned the lenses with the sleeve of her cable-knit cardigan. She glanced down at her sketchbook to see that without thinking, she had begun to outline a scene from a childhood holiday in Dorset. Stood alongside her Gran, with their toes sinking into the sand on the water's edge, both of them with their skirts haphazardly hoisted into their knickers, it was one of those rare moments when all was right with the world.

That was the week when Doris and Lucy had travelled by train to Boscombe on the South Coast and trundled their luggage from the station to their little holiday apartment. The promised sea view was only just visible when you lent your head at the right angle out of the window, but that didn't matter to either of them. Doris had been determined to relax and to spoil her youngest grandchild during this precious time and had carefully arranged respite care for her husband, Will, in order to focus on just that.

The owner of the holiday rental had left a guest welcome pack which generously included homemade scones, strawberry jam and clotted cream alongside the expected milk, sugar and teabags. Taking in their new surroundings, suitcases cast to one side to be dealt with later, they both sank into an armchair to devour the luxury of a cream tea and plot all the adventures that the week might bring. Chips on the beach, a ride on the land train at Hengistbury Head, a visit to the aquarium and more. Lucy could not have guessed then just how poignant this time would become.

Thinking of that week, Lucy let her usual smiling mask slip and quickly rummaged in her bag for another pencil to settle herself again and continue with sketching her beach scene. Like the walls of a sandcastle crumbling before the encroaching tide, Lucy had watched her beloved Gran slowly disappearing to the dementia. It was upsetting to think about what the future might hold and Lucy tried not to dwell on such thoughts but this week it was going to be hard to avoid doing so.

She was struggling to accept the situation but the weekend ahead was marked on the calendar as 'clear out.' The family were all due to descend upon Gran's little house and sort through its contents ahead of viewings. Lucy had argued about the morality of the house sale but could reluctantly see the necessity of releasing funds for the continued care at Green Meadows. Now that Gran had finally settled in there and felt some level of familiarity, nobody wanted to contemplate a move to a more affordable option.

Still, she thought it odd that family members who could not find time to visit Gran from one week to the next, had been able to clear an entire Saturday to sort through her belongings. At least Doris would not be there herself to see what was happening.

4 THE HOUSE CLEARANCE

This was a modest house by many people's standards but without doubt, no matter what other criteria you might use, it had most definitely been a home. The years of care and effort put into maintaining it were matched only by the echoes of family evident within the fabric of this little terraced two-up, two-down. Often seen as the smartest in this East London back street in years gone by, now it stood quietly fading. The proud crimson geraniums long lost to the frosts of several winters, were now overrun by weeds in the front window box. The once scrubbed doorstep was now home to the odd tenacious dandelion and the dust and cobwebs of neglect. When Doris and Will moved in after much scrimping and saving, they had been determined to make the best of their place and if visitors came, they were always warmly welcomed.

Now a developer's eye would view potential, a project of stripping back and knocking through walls to create space with an extended kitchen complete with centre island and sky lights. But pursuing such a project would be a destruction of the essence of this place. For now, until the auction at least, the call of cosy fireside chats beckoned you to the armchair from where your eye could unpick the collection of objects on the cubby-hole shelves. If ever it were possible to capture a lifetime in trinkets, then here Doris was encapsulated.

Her smile radiated from the black and white wedding photograph on the middle shelf – the sort of smile that could light up a room.

Alongside the photograph was a delicate bud vase designed to show off the simplistic beauty of a handful of fresh flowers chosen from the garden as they came into bloom, put to optimum use each year when Will's sweet peas flourished. The care he took to sow, stake and nurture them reaping the rewards of fragrance and colour as an annual treat.

The top shelf had been reserved for items to be kept safely out of reach: a coronation cup and saucer that Doris had kept from her mother's collection of treasures, a small pewter jug of unknown origin, a little wooden box frame made especially to house a couple of aging war medals and, much to Lucy's surprise as she scanned the trinket trove, a pocket-sized pebble. Somewhat out of place on this shelf, this would have no value in an antique shop but Doris had obviously held it in high regard. Lucy recognised it immediately as the pebble from the Dorset beach that she had popped into her bucket and later given to her Gran as she sorted through her other shells and beach finds in the sunshine.

Lucy picked up the pebble and felt the smoothness of it in the palm of her hand. She took a deep breath as she watched the family spread out across the rooms of the house, ready for action. Items were to be sorted into different boxes - sell, throw, or keep. Whilst Lucy's parents and brothers were working out how best to divide their resources, she gave the pebble another squeeze and silently put it into her drawing bag.

"I'm going to have a look upstairs, Dad."

"Okay, Lucy," he replied. "I'll be up in a bit."

She left the others to it and climbed the stairs to see if there were other treasures that she might rescue from the scavenging mission.

In Gran's bedroom was a small hatch into the attic. Perhaps attic is too grand a word for it as in truth the space was too small for any viable room to be made from it. Lucy took a breath and tightened her ponytail before crouching her way through the hatch. She perched herself on one of the cross beams as she allowed her eyes to become accustomed to the half-light within the eaves. To one side was the outline of a shadowy heap which on closer inspection revealed itself to be a couple of old suitcases one on top of another, with a hat box adjacent to them. Lucy wondered when the hat had been worn and how her Gran would have looked, all dressed up in her finery. The thought brought a smile to her face and she used the renewed energy to begin rummaging in a few boxes.

The first box that she peered into was one of Christmas past. Strands of old tinsel entwined with baubles, each one wrapped in tissue paper to preserve them from one year's use to the next. They had a musky smell and the shine of the tinsel had faded. There were some paper lanterns and a couple of concertina-type foil chain decorations that had seen many years of festivities and though old, would probably now be considered retro or 'on trend' in the right setting. A simply carved wooden nativity set was nestled in shredded tissue in its own smaller box, tucked into the bottom corner of this festive treasure trove. Years of use had worn some of the details away but that in itself had its own charm – a simple yet cherished set.

Lucy folded up the top of the box, tucking each flap inside the other to create a closure, wiped her hands on her jeans and moved on. There were a couple of boxes with old clothes in, neatly folded and in mostly good condition. She guessed these would go to the nearest charity shop as they were not the sort of thing that either her mother or her brother's girlfriend, Amy would wear. One chiffon-type scarf caught her eye though and she held it up to take a closer look. There was something about the shade of blue that made Lucy think it was worth holding on to and she folded it carefully to place it into her bag.

A few old board games and jigsaw puzzles were piled on top of a box that had the words 'Train Set' written in faded black ink on the side. Lucy did not recall playing trains in this house and surmised that this set was either bought for her older brothers or was a relic kept from when her father was small. It was hard to imagine him playing with trains or anything really, but she guessed he must have done at some point. Back in the past before work was everything and serious conversations were all he had time for.

She was about to make her way back out of the attic space when she saw something catch the light out of the corner of her eye. Unsure if she was mistaken, she paused to look more carefully. A small Rowntree's Toffee tin had been fitted carefully into a space in the eaves. Lucy thought it looked like the sort of item she had seen for sale in vintage shops in Camden so guessed this tin had been around for a long time. If so, then the contents were most probably significant.

"Lucy, what are you doing up there? I don't want to be here all day, you know. I'm guessing it's mostly junk in there?"

It was her father, hurrying her along as usual and interrupting her thoughts. She did not answer at first, considering what she should do next. She wanted to stay, hidden in the half-dark of the eaves, looking through all the memories for as long as it would take but she knew that would not be possible. She knew also that she did not want to leave the toffee tin there and something told her that she should refrain from sharing her find with the family. If it had been precious enough to have remained stored away for all these years then Lucy knew it was worth hanging on to. She would look inside later.

CHICKENS AND HOPS

(1954)

5 GOLDEN RIDGE FARM

Aunty Joan was a formidable character in her late forties, shaped by farm work and the drive to make ends meet during the war years. With her auburn hair pinned up and hands firmly planted on her hips, she struck an intimidating pose in her crossover pinny. The little farmhouse just outside Faversham in Kent was her domain and she ruled it with a rod of iron. Chores came before frivolity – a term she used to discard any suggestion of a cheerful pursuit. A mantra she had tried to instill in the girls since they had come down from London to stay a while. Doris and Lillian knew better than to argue on this point and completed their allocated chores to the best of their ability. After all, they had been on strict instructions to be on their best behaviour from the moment that Joan had offered to take them in during their mother's long hospital stay.

Their chores were not too bad really and Lillian's sense of adventure had managed to turn many of them into imagined games. So much so that she and Doris would get caught up in the stories at times and quickly had to suppress their giggles for fear of upsetting Aunty Joan. Wash day might involve some serious scrubbing but pegging out the billowing sheets usually incorporated a tale of sail ships, mysterious cargo and faraway lands – often the names of which they had only read from the school atlas but ones that Lillian imagined her stories for and determined she would visit someday.

Mondays were meat pie days and the girls had got quite adept at following their aunt's lead with the mincer that she clamped to the edge of the kitchen table. Turning the handle as if they were performing some magnificent magic trick as they transformed a leftover joint into the filling for a hot meat pie that evening. The meat pie was always Doris' favourite, even if it meant struggling through the limp boiled cabbage that invariably accompanied it upon the plate.

Though the sisters made the best of such tasks, they much preferred the work that took them outside. The early morning forage for mushrooms when the dew clung to the blades of grass and an ethereal mist hung over the fields and they could pretend that they were the only ones left on the planet. Even Lillian could be still and silent for a while when they stood listening to the birdsong and watching the dawn lighting the touch paper of another day. Mushrooms collected and they would be on to the next highlight of their new routine - the daily search for 'golden treasures' in the form of freshly laid eggs in the hen house. Each egg becoming another gemstone in their imaginary jewellery collection – opals, rubies and emeralds. Always with Lillian's bounty winning the day, both for the number of eggs discovered amongst the hay and the fantastical stories she would invent to accompany them.

With Aunty Joan running such a tight ship, the sisters had been quite bewildered when she announced one morning that their chores were cancelled for the rest of the day. Setting a couple of the eggs from the morning haul to poach on the stove, Joan lent against the large kitchen table to explain further.

"I thought you might like a day off, girls. You can take a picnic up to the ridge if you like?"

Lillian let out a squeal which she knew at once would be deemed unladylike but Aunty Joan let it pass. She proceeded to list instructions about their boundaries for the day whilst deftly serving breakfast and making up a picnic at the same time. In light of this unexpected offering, Doris wondered if she had misjudged her aunt a little. Perhaps she was not quite as harsh as the character she presented to the outside world. There was no time to think about this further though as Lillian was chomping at the bit, standing ready at the doorway and promising earnestly to be back in plenty of time for tea. Doris scooped up their basket of provisions and together, the sisters ran off towards the ridge, hand in hand.

They made the most of their freedom that morning, chatting away as they took turns to climb over the stile before running up to the top of the farm ridge.

"Race you to the top, Dottie," called Lillian, setting down the challenge.

"That's not a fair start," Doris replied but Lillian was already out of earshot. There was no point in arguing and Doris trailed behind with the picnic basket. The view beyond the ridge caught them both off guard and they paused from their race to catch their breath and to drink it all in. The verdant patchwork sewn together by the hedgerows, expanding into the distance and closer by, down the other side of the ridge, a cluster of trees to one corner and the glint of water – a stream or river turning a bend and disappearing on its onward journey. It was hard to get a true perspective from their position.

"Come on, Dottie. Let's go take a closer look."

"Guess it can't do any harm."

"I won't tell if you don't," Lillian urged.

"Deal."

Despite their Aunt's warnings to stick to the ridge, the girls had all day before them and decided to explore the riverbank a little before they began their picnic lunch. The sunlight danced on the water, making little patterns as its gentle gurgling entranced anyone who had time to listen. Doris rested their basket against the roots of a sycamore tree and took off her shoes and socks to join Lillian who was already dangling her toes in the cool water. Everything felt slow, the steady flow of the water against their feet, the hovering insects over the river and amongst the reeds at its edges, the gradual warming of their bare arms as the sun beat down upon them. No matter what happened in the future, Doris wanted to remember this day.

Their exploring had built up an appetite so they selected a spot close to the stream to smooth out the tartan blanket and spread out the contents of their picnic basket. There was a sausage roll for each of them – one of Aunty Joan's specialties and one that was impossible to eat without leaving a tell-tale trail of flaky pastry crumbs behind. There were jam sandwiches too, a small chunk of cheese and apples from the orchard. The apples on Golden Ridge Farm were indeed a treat, with a taste far beyond anything the girls could usually manage to pick up from the grocer's stall back home. Then again everything tasted different here, out in the open. Sat in the shade of the sycamore on a day when August was doing its best to host the final flourish of summer, the girls savoured both the tastes and their surroundings.

Lillian was talking of adventures again and planning a long-haul voyage to explore the world once she was old enough to do so. The flecks of light in her cornflower blue eyes flickered as she spoke and her whole being was animated by the promise of discovery and potential. Never one to conform to expectations, usually labelled a bit of a tomboy, there was no doubt that she had the determination to succeed if she put her mind to it. She brushed her hand through her tumble of light brown curls, leaving them more untidy than they already were and demolished the last mouthful of her sausage roll.

Doris knew that all of her sister's stories and imagined adventures were in some way a compensation for never having met her father. Lillian had been conceived during a brief leave from his army duties and was born in 1943, shortly before the dreaded telegram dropped on their doorstep – declared missing in action. Only a few years older herself, Doris had just a few sketchy memories of her father but at least he had known her and had experienced the joy of holding one of his newborn daughters.

Her thought train trailed off along with the shifting shapes in the clouds. She laid back on the grass and felt the sun on her cheeks and drank in the breeze and the buzz of a departing wasp. If only she could fly, she thought, and imagined floating with the clouds. Up and up, over this little slice of English countryside and through an open window to stand alongside a bed. A bed with starched white sheets and a mother's smile that put everything right.

Doris sat bolt upright and refocused her gaze. Her daydream had painted such a vivid image that it both comforted and confused her at the same time. Was her mother alright? Lillian's laughter cut through the moment and Doris smiled back as she saw her sister hanging upside down from a branch of a tree, her feet locking her in place as she swung back and forth.

"Hey, Dottie – let's be pirates!"

Doris hesitated for a moment, feeling that she was beyond her pirate days but then noted the enthusiasm in her sister's plea and decided that she might as well immerse herself in the adventure. Doris was increasingly feeling the pull of the adult world and knew this might well be her last summer of games and flights of fancy. She looked around and retrieved a stick from nearby to hold aloft as she replied

"Arghhh, Lil. Where be the treasure?"

**

After a long afternoon of pirates, exotic wishes and dragon clouds, it was two exhausted girls who now walked along the ridge to make their way back to the farmhouse. Soon this space would be dotted with little white tents to house the hop pickers. The numbers making their way from London to set themselves up for the harvest weeks had dwindled over the past few years, as the process was being taken over by machinery. But Golden Ridge Farm still needed some help with their hops and anticipated the usual disruption to routine that happened each year.

The girls looked each other up and down, as they reached the hen house. What a sorry sight they were – especially Lillian. She had grass stains on her skirt and muddy knees. Her sleeves were rolled up to her elbows and she looked like she would need a week in the tin bath and a good hard scrub with carbolic soap to ever look clean again. Stood alongside Aunty Joan's regimented hollyhocks and marigolds, they wondered what response they would get once they went inside and could no longer suppress their desire to giggle.

It was at that very moment that Aunty Joan chose to appear in the doorway and called to them.

"Girls, there you are. I was starting to worry."

"Sorry, Aunty Joan," Doris managed to reply between giggles. "We lost track of time."

"What on earth do you look like?" Joan scalded.

The girls tried not to look at each other for fear that it would make the giggling worse so instead they focused their gaze steadfastly on their feet.

"Never mind girls, we'll sort that all out later. We've got a guest for tea and I think you'll be pleased to see her."

Joan stepped to one side and slowly emerging from the kitchen, the girls saw a face they'd been longing to see for the past two months. A brief moment of realisation passed between them before both girls shrieked as they dropped the picnic remains and ran towards the doorway.

"Mum!"

6 THE DANCE HALL

Sunday afternoon, a time when shops shut and the bustle of life stopped. Recently Doris had come to regard this time as her favourite part of the week. It was two years now since the day of the picnic on Golden Ridge Farm and the period of convalescence that had extended for several months there, with Aunty Joan at the helm. Now Doris and Lillian could see that their mother, Daisy, was slowly returning to being the woman that they both knew and cherished and all three of them were pleased to finally be back in their own home.

Dinner and dishes done, Sunday afternoons allowed for a couple of lazy hours, an oasis of time to rest from the usual daily routines of the rest of the week. Lillian would take to her reading, knees bent up on her chair propping up her chosen book, she would devour any content that she could lay her hands on. The local library, any jumble sales and the secondhand book stall in the local street market had become her regular haunts, as well as eager book swaps with anyone from the neighbourhood who would join her. There were always a few books on the little shelf by her bed, demanding her attention whenever time allowed her to devote it.

Whilst Daisy dozed in the armchair, with her feet propped up in front of the little coal fire, Doris would invariably turn her attention to the old mahogany piano. The fading ivory keys had seen many melodies played out over the years but now they only responded to Doris' fingers. She had never had the luxury of formal lessons but had picked up her skill over time from watching her mother, until such time that Daisy's illness had left her too weak to focus on playing.

Doris had a good ear and played a mixture of tunes that she had heard on the radio. Many of the songs that she had grown up hearing at family gatherings fell into her repertoire, with her tinkling the keys until over time, she had worked out their accompaniments and she and Lillian could sing along. By no means an accomplished pianist but she enjoyed playing for pleasure and recently had started to play for a few shillings at their local pub, The Eight Bells. It was a happy diversion from her day job and household chores and as she played, she found herself adopting a different, more carefree persona. The music gave her a confidence that usually eluded her.

She played for quite a while that afternoon, filling the time between dinner and their usual Sunday tea of shrimps and winkles bought from Stan's barrow on the corner of their street, where the local kids played hopscotch or sang 'Over the Garden Wall,' between the rebounding balls of their games. As her fingers loosened up, Doris let herself relax into her playing and allowed her mind to merge with the music. She could picture herself on a film set, tossing her shoulder-length hair flirtatiously as the leading man sauntered over and asked her to strike up another tune whilst he poured their drinks from a well-stocked bar.

It struck Doris that both she and her sister relied heavily upon their imaginations, the characters and scenes that they created from their music and stories to escape the mundane and reality of their little lives. It would be a little moment, a simple thing that would change the direction of that life that very week.

***

"See you Monday, Maureen."

Doris was finishing her shift at Woolworths and as usual had a couple of errands to run on the way home. Before leaving the store, she picked up a bag of broken biscuits and dashed to the nearby heel bar for a revamp of her dancing shoes, ready for the evening. She enjoyed her work in the store, helping to keep her counter in top condition, and had gained confidence in talking to the customers. Doris was blossoming from the shy, hardworking girl of her school days into a young woman, slowly embracing the steps of independence that she had begun to discover. Her simple clothes and the way she fixed her hair may have been plain and functional, but there was no denying the attraction of the kindness of her smile.

On her way to the pie and mash shop she decided to make a small diversion to pop into the little record store on the corner of Faraday Street and thumbed her way through the records on the shelves. The song of the day, 'Que Sera Sera' by her namesake, Doris Day, was playing regularly on the radio and she loved singing along, wondering what her own future might be. As she listened to the music within the record booth and looked around the store she felt an energy and excitement growing within. That evening she was going to the dance hall where each week some of the local bands played the latest tunes.

She had been pleasantly surprised when her mother had given her permission to go and was looking forward to catching the bus later with her two friends, Molly and Liz. They were both a little older than Doris, and Daisy had been satisfied that they would all look out for each other. As long as she was home by 10.30pm – everything would be fine.

She tore herself away from the thrill of looking at all the records and the promised joy of the music within their sleeves and carried on down Faraday Street. Just past the sarsaparilla stall, stood the pie and mash shop, waiting to draw in its customers from the cold. This was not a weekly treat, but on some Saturdays Doris would collect pie, mash and liquor for the three of them and together they would revel in its hot comfort.

Today though, she would not linger too long over her meal and instead wanted to devote her time to getting ready for the dance. She cleared the plates and began fixing her hair. This was going to be a rare treat. Lillian may have been teasing her a little but Doris knew it was only in jest and also because she was just a little jealous not to be old enough to join in the adventure. After all they had always done so much together. Many times the sisters had danced at family birthdays or at Christmas when there were so many relatives crammed together in one room that there was barely space to move. Even so, after eating the festive meal the trestle tables would be packed away and music found to entertain and those who were not sleeping off the excesses of the day, would find their toes tapping and the dancing beginning.

Now, the sisters listened to their little radiogram and talked of the tunes that Doris might dance to that evening.

"I wish I could come too."

"There'll be plenty of other dances, when you're a bit older."

"Guess so. Make sure you tell me all about it though."

"I'll do my best. Now, how do I look?"

She was almost ready and smoothed out the pale green skirt of her best dancing dress.

"You'll do," said Lillian, helping Doris to fix the final pin in her roll of hair. "Just a touch of lipstick, then you'll be perfect." She got the balance just right, not enough lipstick for mother to raise an eyebrow over but just enough to add interest. Doris checked her bag for the third time.

"Time to go then."

Doris met her friends on the corner and the three of them chatted and giggled excitedly for the whole bus ride to the dance. After paying their ticket price at the door, they walked arm in arm into the little dance hall. In a setting that had seen fox trots and waltzes, lindy hops and jives, the girls all looked their best in their dancing dresses, petticoat layers protruding slightly from beneath them and were ready to swirl their way through the evening as the tunes progressed. Though they started the evening very much chatting and dancing together, it did not take long before they were noticed by some of the men in the room who joined the three girls in conversation.

Doris had not taken too much notice of the attention being paid to them until at one moment, mid-way through a particularly good skiffle number, she turned to see that one particular man had his gaze fixed firmly in her direction. He was a tall, broad shouldered man with Brylcreem slicked-back blonde hair and soft hazel eyes. She no longer heard the music playing or saw what anyone else in the room was doing. He approached her and confidently took her hand to ask

"May I have this dance?"

For the rest of the evening, Will and Doris danced and chatted as if they had always known each other. The time tumbled away until Doris suddenly realised how late it had got and panicked that she would be in trouble if she did not get off to the bus stop quickly. Liz and Molly were having too good a time to break away from their fun just yet and tried to persuade her to stay a little longer but Will, sensing her unease, offered to escort her home.

It was raining heavily when Doris and Will left the dance hall to dash for the bus stop. It did not matter to either of them. They held hands as they dodged the puddles, laughing when they occasionally misjudged their step and sent splashes cascading up their legs. On reaching the bus stop, Will noticed that Doris had begun to shiver and took off his coat to wrap around her shoulders in the first of many protective gestures that she would come to love over the years ahead.

Against the darkness, the falling rain was highlighted by the lamplight and Doris felt Will's arm tighten around her waist. She leaned her head against his shoulder and wished that she could stay in this perfect moment forever as her bus slowly came into view.

UNRAVELLING

FAMILY TIES

(2015)

7 TOFFEE TREASURES

Lucy's bedroom might be the smallest one in the extended semi-detached house but it was her own space to sort as she wanted, free from the opinions of the rest of the family. And it was true to say that her family were not slow to express their opinions. She had been thinking a lot about the meaning of family lately, how some family members felt like people that you just had to put up with whilst there were others that you shared a stronger bond with, yet either way, you were tied to all of them. Whether they be in your life much or not, both past and present, family ties stretching across the years. Of course, in all of this Gran remained central to her thoughts. The bond between them remained strong in spite of Gran's struggle with her illness.

Lucy had a good idea about many of the branches of Gran's family tree from the information she had managed to piece together over time. Stories from both her Gran and other relatives had scattered their seeds through Lucy's mind over time and grown into her perceptions of what life looked like for the various relatives in the stories. There was also a box of old family photos that helped her to bring such tales to life.

Shortly after their week's holiday in Boscombe, when she found herself saying her last goodbye to her Granddad, Lucy had spent a quiet, rainy afternoon looking through the box of photos with Gran. It was during one of those long days that follow the funeral of a loved one when the waves of grief hit hard. The two of them had sipped tea together and found the distraction of the assorted images served as a good distraction, even allowing a smile or two to spread between them as shared moments were recalled. Afterwards, Lucy had been allowed to bring the box home as long as she promised to look after its contents and she felt honoured to be entrusted with its care.

She had made room for it on her bookshelf, alongside her many books. Many times she had been told that she was following in her Great Aunt Lillian's footsteps. Just like her, Lucy could lose herself in a book for hours at a time. Often she would read in bed until the early hours, lighting the pages from beneath her duvet with the light from a little torch. Though she read a great many genres, as reflected in her eclectic collection stacked upon her bookcase, she had developed a love of history and read many works of historical fiction just to immerse herself in scenes of eras past. She loved the feeling of walking alongside the characters, wondering what it would be like if she could just step off the pages and into their world in a different time and place to her own.

Lucy had a shelf of novels which included stories from the past, tales of fantasy and strange new worlds, several classics that she had studied at school or discovered on her English teacher's recommendation. There was also a shelf where her childhood favourites remained alongside design books, art history and a magazine holder that housed a variety of art papers waiting to be used in one craft project or another. It was fair to say that art and reading filled her life.

Lucy's eldest brother, Tom, was nine years old when she was born and the twins, Harry and James, were five. Although the only girl and thus many might expect the recipient of much over indulgence, in fact her birth had been a bit of an inconvenience to her parents who had just got to the point when all their children were to be in school and they were poised to move forward with their careers. Her mother, Jane, had gone so far as to say that she had been an unexpected surprise and there were several times when Lucy wondered if that was really code for an unwanted development in the family dynamic.

Lucy thought about that as she opened the pages of her current project, a journal where she was scrapbooking the family story that kept forming in her head. She thought that some of her sketches from Green Meadows might find a place alongside the other family details she planned to document. On the first page she had drawn a beautiful swirling family tree with miniature portraits like the sort usually found within an old fashioned locket. Most of the portraits she had either created from direct observation or from the photographs in Gran's box, where she could find ones to match the relatives she had never met. Further back in time was more problematic and here, Lucy had let her imagination and developing historical knowledge fill in the gaps. She was hoping the day's attic finds would give her inspiration for further pages of her journal.

She had managed to wait for a convenient time to return to the toffee tin. The day of sorting had been long and upsetting and involved much organisation in the division of duties, one car taking items designated for charity donation, another the belongings deemed worthy enough to hold on to, whilst much of the other house contents were piled into the skip that had been booked for the weekend. After such a draining day, the family had picked up a takeaway and slouched on the sofa with full stomachs and aching limbs. Lucy knew she would not be missed from the banal television viewing and escaped to the sanctuary of her bedroom for the rest of the evening.

She looked at the contents of her drawing bag, spread out across her little wooden desk, the space where she drew and painted. Moving her jar of paintbrushes to one side, she unfolded the scarf and decided that she would take it to Green Meadows next week and give it to Gran. The colour would complement Gran's eyes and she might like to wear it on occasion, perhaps when taking a little walk around the gardens there.

The pebble was next and Lucy picked a suitable spot for it on her bookcase. She already had a few natural objects on one shelf - shells and a small piece of driftwood from beach trips, a few twigs tied in a piece of twine from a time when she had imagined the need for a magic wand, a peacock feather and some crystal rocks that she had bought in a museum souvenir shop. The pebble would fit well in that spot.

"Now," said her inner voice, "what has Gran kept in here for all of these years?"

She took off the lid of the tin and tentatively peered inside. On top was a pile of postcards and letters held together by a piece of ribbon that had been lovingly tied into a bow. Lucy undid the bow and thought at first that they might be old love letters from her Granddad or perhaps another secret flame. But as she began to read the first few she realized that they were in fact letters from Lillian, detailing places and events from a wide range of destinations.

Lucy knew that Lillian had ended up living abroad but did not know quite how many places she had been to. The odd parts of conversations she had heard placed alongside the different postcards and letters began to combine into a lifetime of adventure and Lucy was fascinated. She would love to have met her Great Aunt and knew she would return to reading these little parts of her life again and again. For now, curiosity to examine the rest of the tin's contents prompted her to put the correspondence to one side and to wait for a time when she might not be quite so tired and could give each letter the full attention that it deserved.

Returning to the tin, Lucy retrieved a fading envelope and opened it to find a bus ticket. It was a strange item for somebody to keep but Lucy gave a little audible gasp as she discovered it. Many a time her Gran had talked about the night she had met the man who would become her husband. The kind man who had warmed her with his coat and talked of his work as a gardener. Lucy knew the tale of the bus ride in the rain well, when Gran had popped her ticket from the bus conductor safely into her purse and proceeded to keep it within the pages of her diary as a souvenir of the night they had first danced together. Gran got the details of the story confused now, but Lucy remembered them, along with other moments that Gran would share during many story times.

Lucy put the ticket back into the envelope and placed it into her desk drawer for safekeeping. Then she looked into the tin once more to see if anything else remained. At the base of the tin, there were two items wrapped in tissue paper and Lucy picked them up. She unwrapped the first, to reveal a silver brooch, shaped like a branch with green glass stones in the shape of leaves dotted along it. A piece of vintage costume jewellery, simple yet pretty. Stored away out of sight for how many years? Lucy wondered when it had last adorned a hat or coat and why it had been kept here and not alongside her Gran's other jewellery.

She wrapped it back up and moved onto the next package. Inside was a discovery that also puzzled her – a pair of white knitted booties, pinned together with a small loop of pink ribbon. They looked like they had never been used. She wondered if they could have been hers but if so, Lucy could not think why Gran might have them and why she would have placed them in this toffee tin time capsule. They must have belonged to some other baby girl.

Perhaps she should ask Gran? Would Gran remember any of these items now? It was always hard to tell how conversations about the past would go with her. She decided against it for now and wrapped the booties back up and placed them and the pretty brooch back into the tin, after all that had been their home for a long time.

8 SWEET DREAMS

"You need to go back to bed now, Doris" said Linda. "It's almost midnight."

Linda was the care manager on duty that night and had tried twice already to help Doris back to her bedroom. This time Doris had got as far as the front lobby which was quite the achievement without her walking frame. With that in mind, Linda was keen to avoid Doris taking a fall as she stood between her and the front door.

"Come on now, Doris. That's enough dancing for tonight."

"Just a little dance."

"Not for me, thanks."

"Have you seen my husband? He's taking me to the dance hall, you know."

Doris frequently asked for Will and was mostly confused by the answers she received. Most days she waited for him to come home from work and tell her all about his day and the blooms he had tended. She frequently told the care staff about his green fingered skills and how he loved his work in the gardens, even being out in all weathers, connecting with nature.

"Flowers never argue with you," recounted Doris "Will always says that."

"That's very true," Linda replied.

"Always in the garden, Will."

"Making it beautiful, I'm sure."

By now, Linda had managed to distract Doris from her dancing and was now supporting her under the arm as she slowly steered her away from the lobby to take the lift to the first floor and make their way along the lamp lit corridor. Linda had worked at Green Meadows for many years and was a mixture of efficiency and goodwill. She was a rather plump woman with an honest face. The greying roots of her hair showed amongst the vibrant shades of red that she chose to add when time permitted. Time was something that she did not have a lot of, between her family commitments and regular night shifts.

"Here we are now, Doris, back in your room. Let me sort your pillows for you," said Linda in a way that was both firm and kind as she quickly arranged the pillows and the bedclothes for Doris. She hoped that Doris would settle now and helped her to take off her pink quilted housecoat. She hung it on the hook on the wall and then held Doris under both elbows to help her lower herself onto the bed.

"Time for some beauty sleep now, you can do some more dancing in the morning." A reassuring smile spread across Linda's face, masking its weariness as she manoeuvred each of Doris' swollen feet out of their pale green Marks and Spencer's slippers. Taking her time, she listened to Doris telling her about her wedding day, even though she had heard her tell similar stories several times before.

"Sweet dreams then, Doris."

Linda left the nightlight on and backed out of the room, relieved that Doris seemed to be finally settling down under her cover, and tentatively closed the bedroom door.

As Doris allowed her head to rest on her pillow, she drifted into that halfway place between dreams and the end of the day. Shadows played around the room and her mind but slowly her breathing began to settle into a more relaxed rhythm. Sleep beckoned and within it, Doris was young again.

***

She was stood at the top of a set of white polished steps outside a church and Lillian was by her side. They had both tamed their curls into beehive hairstyles after much determined backcombing and copious amounts of hairspray, each one demarcated with an Alice band. Lillian's was made with dusky pink ribbon, matching the dress she wore whilst Doris wore a more elaborate beaded white one, with a length of simple white tulle secured behind it. Both held small bouquets filled with flowers that Will had tended and supplied for the wedding day and the fragrance of the soft pink roses hung in the air. Doris took a deep breath, "What do you think?"

"You look beautiful," said Lillian.

"Thank-you."

Lillian gave her sister's arm a little squeeze, "This is your day, Dottie, enjoy it. Today you're a princess like the ones in my old story books."

They stood facing each other, children no longer and they both felt a passing moment of sadness for this loss. Doris was now twenty-one and Lillian, at the age of seventeen, was turning a few heads of her own. Two confident young women who had been through so much together now stood, without either parent alive to see them, waiting for Wagner's Bridal Chorus to strike up on the church organ. The music began playing and drew the sisters away from their moment of reflection, to walk down the aisle where the congregation waited eagerly to celebrate Doris and Will's marriage.

Afterwards the happy couple and all their guests posed for photographs, sharing smiles and laughter on a sunny June day before all heading to The Eight Bells to dance into the night. The landlord, Jim, and his wife, Betty, had been very generous, laying on much of the party as their wedding gift to the happy couple. They had a soft spot for Doris, ever since she had started playing piano there several years ago, compounded by a determination to look out for her and her sister when they heard of Daisy's passing, even offering them digs in a room above the pub. So it was down to their generosity that the bar was lined up with trays of sandwiches, vol-au-vents and sausage rolls.

"To the happy couple," beamed Jim. "Bottoms up!"

The whole atmosphere in the pub was one of goodwill as both the drinks and the evening flowed on. Looking around, there were some glasses bubbling with Babycham, others raised a cherry brandy or a gin and tonic in celebration whilst many clutched their beer glass to toast and frequently refilled it. Clearly there would be more than a few sore heads in the morning.

There was talk of Lillian being next and jest about who would be the lucky guy to see her as the bride instead of the bridesmaid, but Lillian had other ideas. Their childhood games might be a thing of the past but she still had a spirit of adventure burning strongly within her. She might not know yet how it was going to happen but Lillian was determined to start her travels. This evening was not the time for such talk though. It was Doris and Will's special night, full of singing and dancing, laughter and chatting, wishes for their future, happiness and long life. Lillian picked up another egg and cress sandwich and raised her Babycham towards them with the sincere hope that all would be well on their future road together.

9 SHADES OF BLUE

Andrew was on his mobile phone in the next room when parts of his conversation began to interrupting Lucy's drawing. She had returned to her beach sketch to add further details and planned to use her new brush tipped pens to bring the colours of the treasured memory to life. With money saved up from her last few pay days Lucy had treated herself to an hour in her favourite art shop, browsing the shelves and selecting the best materials that her budget would allow for. Her new brush pens could give the appearance of a watercolour finish when carefully applied and Lucy had fanned out the selection of pens in front of her in anticipation of an evening of drawing.

"I'm sorry to hear that, does she need a review of her medication?"

Her father must have been talking to the nursing home. They called occasionally to keep him informed of developments in Gran's care, to answer any queries he may have made about their finance plan and sometimes to ask if he was planning to visit that month.

"I'm not sure I'm going to be able to make it this weekend. I'm snowed under at work and we've been trying to sort the house sale... Yes, I understand. I'll see if I can move things around... Yes, thank you. Oh yes, I'm sure that Lucy will be along tomorrow as usual. I'll let her know."

Lucy paused with her cobalt pen mid-brushstroke and waited to hear if there was any further conversation. She wondered what had prompted the call from Green Meadows and asked herself why it was that her father was so caught up in his work that he could not drop everything to go and sort Gran himself. Her father was a business driven man and a creature of habit. He had worked his way up in the firm over the last twenty years wearing this loyalty like a badge of honour, often telling people that it was most unusual these days for anyone to stay in the same place of work for more than a few years. Perhaps it would have done him good to change jobs a little and gain a wider perspective but Lucy was not going to suggest that, she knew her comments would be dismissed as naïve and she would be told that she was too young to know anything about the business world.

Consequently, every weekday, her father would leave the house early in the morning to make the fifteen minute walk to Blackheath station, ready to catch the 7.03 to Victoria. Lucy was unsure what he exactly did when he got to the offices but she knew it involved spreadsheets and conference calls and regular coffees from the staff canteen. He routinely ate at his desk unless he had clients to meet over a lunch at the nearest pub, always put on the company expenses. After such days he would get back home at about 8pm, hastily eat his evening meal and either look at some papers from his work bag or perhaps watch some television programme or another from behind dozing eyelids. Most of his conversation was limited to passing comments on his way in and out of the house, until the weekends when there always seemed to be something that he needed to do. Lucy's overriding impression of her father was that he never had time for her.

She heard him knock on the bedroom door and turned around in her swiveling desk chair to see him come in.

"What are you drawing there, Lucy?" he asked as he perched himself awkwardly on the edge of her bed, pushing his glasses back into place on the bridge of his nose.

"Oh it's nothing much, just a beach scene," she replied.

"Ah, that's nice."

He waited a moment, hesitant to continue, perhaps considering what to say next and in the silence, Lucy tried unsuccessfully to recall the last time that he had asked her about her artwork.

"Oh, um," he began, twisting his wedding ring on his finger, "Are you going to see Gran tomorrow?" he continued.

"Of course, I go every Tuesday."

"Yes, yes you do."

His words floated in the room without direction as his gaze moved from Lucy to somewhere in the middle distance. A long pause passed before he continued.

"It's very good of you to do that, to keep in touch all the time like that. I would go more if…" he broke off his sentence and looked down at the floor.

For the first time, Lucy felt a little sorry for her father. She had a sudden urge to give him a hug but thought better of it because she did not know how he would respond to such spontaneous affection. They had never been a hugging family. Instead, she spoke for him in an attempt to ease the tension.

"It's okay, you have a lot to think about with your work."

"Yes, things have been busy, still…"

"I like to check in on Gran anyway. It's a good place to sit and draw, at Green Meadows, once she settles into her storytelling."

Lucy smiled and waited for a response. It was as if her father had been waiting for permission to talk about Gran and that all this time that he had said nothing, he had been keeping all his thoughts safely tucked up under lock and key. In the ten minutes or so that followed, with the awkward exchange exposing his vulnerabilities, Lucy made a connection that she had not felt before.

They talked about how Gran's condition was getting worse, how she had been taking longer at nights to settle in her room and that Lucy should be prepared for her to be more confused as time goes on. He promised Lucy that he would try to be better at making time to go and see his mother, "I'll be a bit more organized, Lucy, so I can pop in."

"I'm sure Gran will like that."

"Yeah, she might even recognise me next time. Maybe?"

Lucy wanted to be able to reassure him though they both knew this was highly unlikely. She held his gaze and then found her answer, "On the inside. I'm sure she knows who we all are."

Then as quickly as their conversation had begun, Andrew stood to make an exit.

"I'm off to put the kettle on, do you want anything?"

"No thanks, Dad. Not just yet."

As he made his way off to the kitchen, Lucy felt the familiar sting behind the eyes that takes hold to stifle a cry. She wanted so much to be able to do more, to have some control over this cruel battle. She looked to the familiarity of her belongings in the room to quell the unsettled feeling stirring in her mind.

On her desk before her, the new cobalt blue pen lay alongside the beach scene, waiting to bring the waves and the sky to life. Lucy imagined the blue colour washing over her and remembered Gran's chiffon scarf from her attic finds. Taking several slow, deliberate breaths, she could picture it floating on a breeze across the beach scene on her desk. She went over to the chest of drawers in the corner of her room.

Each drawer had different patterned handles, chosen from a collection she had made over time, rummaging in the local charity shop. Absentmindedly twiddling the round mauve and white floral ones on the top drawer she stood for a moment before opening the drawer to retrieve the scarf from alongside her other clothes there. She pulled it through her fingers, allowing its softness to linger against her skin and sat on her bed lost in the silence of her thoughts.

When her attention drifted back to her room, she circled her shoulders a few times to ease the tension within them and gave the open top drawer a firm push. Lucy folded the scarf into a neat square and slipped it into her drawing bag. She would give it to Gran tomorrow and all would be fine.

PASTE AND POSTCARDS

(1963)

10 BREWER STREET

Walking down Brewer Street this evening, passers-by would have been forgiven for thinking that there was a party going on at number 53. They would certainly have heard music playing and the sounds of laughter periodically coming from the open window of the front room. The picture inside though was not one of a typical party scene.

It is true that there were several 45s stacked on the arm of the Dansette record player, ready to drop into place as each of the previous tunes ended. And it is true that those gathered in the room were singing along to them but there was not much time or space for dancing there. Instead of party food and glasses clinking, there was a pasting table in the centre of the room, a ladder against one wall, a bucket of paste with a large brush dipped into it and several rolls of wallpaper. Doris and Will had enlisted help in their endeavor to make their house into the home they had been dreaming of. Tonight this help took the form of a 'decorating party.'

Will's brother, Fred, was there and he appeared to be a dab hand at pasting and folding the saffron and pea green floral wallpaper that was going to breathe fresh life into their front room. The trick was getting the pattern to line up whilst there was still enough slide in the paste to move each drop of wallpaper around. Will had managed to get a good deal on the paper through a friend in the trade but even so, he had barely enough rolls and could ill afford to waste any on mistakes. Thus he and Fred were trying hard to hang the paper with great precision. They were getting into the swing of it now and had the process of pasting, folding and hanging each drop, down to a fine art.

Lillian was quite happy with her designated painting task and danced along to the music with her paintbrush in her hand, joining in with the lyrics here and there.

"We'll do the twist, the stomp, the mashed potato too…"

"Any old dance that you wanna do," joined in Doris, "But let's dance."

"Oi, Missus! Not too much dancing for you," called Will from the top of the ladder. "Take it easy, love."

"I'm okay, stop fussing," Doris replied. She liked that he was looking out for her though and took a little breather from painting the windowsill to prop her feet up for a bit. She had noticed that they had been swelling more easily, the longer that the pregnancy went on. In the end she had to admit defeat and gave up on the painting. She sat as comfortably as she could make herself and surveyed the scene before her, to check on the progress of everyone else.

Their next-door-neighbour, Maggie, who had only popped round on the pretence of borrowing some sugar, took over the job that Doris had started and stayed all evening. Maggie was a couple of years older than Doris and still living at home with her Mam, 'Irish Mary' – as she was affectionately called by the other neighbours on Brewer Street. It had not taken Doris and Will long to get to know Maggie.

She had turned up on their doorstep the day after they moved in, with a loaf of soda bread freshly baked for them. Without pausing to catch her breath, she had given the couple the lowdown on all the nearest neighbours, told them how grand it was to have somebody new on the street and explained that her Mam made the soda bread every week, as a little bit of Ireland and that there was nothing else quite like it. Still warm, with a generous helping of butter spread on it, Irish Mary's gift had been a welcome start to their life in their new home.

Doris decided that Maggie and Lillian were as good as each other at filling a gap in a conversation and between their chatter and the singing along to the records that evening, the house was filled with a tangible buzz of positive energy. The cooperation of family and friends can achieve great things and though the job may have been tiring, they all worked cheerfully until it was almost midnight. At that point, Doris emerged from the kitchen with a tray for all, containing cups of tea and a pile of hot, buttered crumpets.

"Time to down tools," she announced.

"No argument from me there," said Will.

Between them they had more or less finished the room and Will and Fred were quick to clear away the pasting table and bucket so that all could find a free surface to sit down and tuck into their tray of rewards. Rewards that made a welcome midnight snack. They congratulated each other on a job well done and with the music now turned off, sank into the sort of cosy conversation that comes easily between friends. Between the sips of tea and buttery mouthfuls they chatted about their lives and plans, with much of the conversation centered on the couple's home and the impending arrival of its newest resident.

It had taken a lot of saving and a fair amount of good luck to secure this house and make this start together, away from their cramped conditions squashed in with Will's family. Though grateful to them, both Will and Doris were keen to have their own space and make it into the home they wanted, even if Brewer Street was only a few streets away. Will regularly popped back to his family home to see his parents and Fred who seemed in no hurry to leave the nest. Although Fred was Will's older brother by five years, in many ways they were quite similar. Both kind, with broad smiles and eyes that danced when they laughed. They were both practical men, able to turn their hands to any odd job that cropped up and Fred had been happy to support Will and Doris whenever he could.

As the conversation meandered on it was Fred who was first to notice that Doris had nodded off to sleep and he nudged Will and stood up to announce "Think that's our cue to go, come on Maggie I'll escort you home, it's on my way."

"Ah that'll be grand," she giggled.

It was all of a few steps to her doorstep but she took the hint and grabbed her coat, whilst Will thanked them both for all their help and then closed the door behind them. Lillian gathered up the cups, stacked them on the tea tray and returned them to the kitchen. She was staying over for the weekend and busied herself washing the cups before sorting out her blanket and pillow for the put-you-up bed in the spare room. Will had already carried Doris upstairs and after such a long and exhausting evening it would not be long until the whole house would fall into the silence of slumber.

As Lillian tried to make herself comfortable, she looked around the lamp lit spare room – soon to become a child's bedroom. Her storytelling mind conjured up a scene before her of a cot, broken silences and night feeds. New babies have no regard for the lateness of the hour and there were but a few weeks left until her sister would be managing feeds and tears and nappies. She knew that Doris would make a great mother, after all she had shared much of that role whilst they were growing up and for that, Lillian would always be grateful. She smiled and turned off the lamp wondering if the bedroom would be for a niece or a nephew. They would all know soon enough and she would wait to be an Aunt for a little while before beginning her great adventure.

11 CHRISTMAS EVE

It was a Christmas of firsts. Most notably, the first one as a family of three. Andrew was almost eight months old by the time Will and Doris were hanging up paper chains in their front room and balancing a handmade angel on top of their little artificial tree. They both doted on Andrew and so too did the stream of visitors who popped in to coo at him in the cot and comment upon how much he had grown. The couple were grateful for the support and attention from family, friends and neighbours and were always willing to give guests their time and cups of tea as they welcomed them into their home. However much this was true, there was one visitor that Doris really wished could be there – her mother, Daisy.

She felt her loss more acutely during the first few months of being a mother herself and she craved the advice that is usually passed down from one generation to the next. Grief always shows its face more openly at such significant dates and times over the years and Doris reflected upon how cruel a twist of fate it had been for her mother to have caught that winter flu, when she had managed to make such a recovery from the tuberculosis. There had been just too many odds stacked against her. Doris sighed deeply, telling herself to focus upon the here and now and started peeling the potatoes for dinner as she listened to the Beatles playing on Radio Caroline.

This Christmas was also the first one that Doris would not be sharing with Lillian. She stood by the sink drainer with her peeler at the ready, picturing how the two of them would have been dancing together in her kitchen, had Lillian been there. Instead, many miles distance lay between the two sisters this Christmas Eve, two sisters who had been inseparable for most of their lives. Shortly after Andrew's birth, Lillian had announced her travel plans and within weeks was off to catch the boat train from Victoria to Paris.

Lillian had squirrelled away savings ever since she first had any earnings, helping out on a local market stall. After leaving school, she had taken any work she could until she had accrued a modest amount of money. This was her travelling fund and now she was ready to use it to set off on all the adventures that she had always wanted to have. She planned to work her way from one place to another, wherever fate may take her.

Doris might have understood the reasons behind Lillian's decision and had every faith that Lillian would make a success of it but she was always going to worry about her 'little sister.' In reality, that had been her role for many years. All that was swirling in her head as she stood beside Lillian on the platform that evening. Doris had determined to put on a brave face but many tears were shed when it was time to wave Lillian on her way, with her hopes and dreams packed alongside her clothes in her suitcase.

Doris admired her sister's adventurous spirit and had always known that Lillian could not be contained in one place for it would be like pinning a butterfly by its wing. Now, Doris had her own life story unfolding with her little family in Brewer Street. Serving up a simple dinner of cold meat and boiled potatoes, surrounded by the love of a happy home, Doris thought how lucky she and her sister had been to have kind people in their lives. She watched Andrew kicking his legs in his carry cot and she wondered what his future would look like, then chided herself for getting all sentimental.

"Penny for 'em?" Will asked.

"Uh, sorry love. Thoughts running away with me, that's all," she replied.

"Lillian?"

"Yes. I hope she's alright, Will."

"She'll be fine, Dot, I'm sure. Reckon she'll be raising a glass somewhere and chatting ten to the dozen."

Will always knew instinctively what Doris was thinking and more importantly, what to say to make her feel better.

"I'll clear this lot, they'll be in from next door soon."

"Thanks, love. I'll take this little man up to his room."

She took Andrew upstairs whilst Will started clearing away the dinner things. Both jobs done, they each returned to the front room. Maggie and Irish Mary were joining them for a drink before they went on to midnight mass later. Will had invited them for a festive sherry and thought that it would be nice for Doris, as he had guessed she would be missing Lillian. Doris knew that she really could not have found a more generous and thoughtful man and was looking forward to joining his family the next day for what promised to be quite the festive feast. Although she would be helping out in the kitchen of course, along with Will's mother and sister, Polly, she was quietly relieved not to be hosting the Christmas dinner as there would definitely not have been room for all his family in their little two up, two down.

Maggie burst into the room with her usual vibrancy but turned up a notch, if that were possible, by virtue of the fact that it was Christmas Eve.

"Isn't this just lovely? So nice of you to invite us." Maggie was triumphant in her announcement of their presence as she and Mary took off their coats.

"Let me take those, Maggie." Will hung the coats up as Maggie continued.

"Thankyou. We'll certainly need those later, bound to freeze on our way to Mass, eh Mam?" Maggie's smile beamed across the room as Mary nodded in reply, anticipating that Maggie would not be pausing for any further response to her comment and made herself comfortable in one of the armchairs.

"I love Christmas Eve, don't you, Dottie? Mam and I get all dressed up in our church best and now we get to share it with you, well isn't that just the cherry on the cake? And it looks so pretty in here."

"Yes, Maggie. 'Tis grand, for sure," said Irish Mary, taking in the details of the decorated room from her vantage point in the corner.

Will and Doris exchanged a glance and both smiled earnestly. Will managed to chip in quick, as Maggie took a breath to look around the room, "Sherry, ladies?"

"Yes please," gushed Maggie, "and for you, Mam?"

"Oh yes, that'll hit the spot."

Will was already opening the bottle from the sideboard ready to pour into the little sherry glasses, each one a different colour, each one catching the light to cast its own glow. He put down the Harvey's Bristol Cream bottle and passed around the glasses.

"Cheers everyone."

A chorus echoing the cheers followed and then Mary added "May Santa put something good in your stocking!"

They all started laughing at this remark, until baby Andrew's cries signaled that he was in need of a little more attention before he would settle for the night. Doris went upstairs and her soft lullaby floated down to the sherry drinkers below. It did not take too long for him to settle. Too young to sense the festive excitement of gifts to come on Christmas Day, there would be plenty of times ahead for that.

When Doris returned to the front room, Maggie was in full flow again, chatting away to explain that she and her mam had brought them round a tin of Rowntree's toffees as a little appreciation for being such fine neighbours.

"We'll just have to open that now then and share a few," said Doris, "thank you, it's such a pretty tin."

She passed the tin around and the conversation paused for long enough for each of them to chew on their chosen toffee and wash it down with a few sips of sherry. It was a cosy scene, one of neighbours who had become firm friends. They sat together beneath the paper chains with the smell of mince pies wafting through from the oven and talked of Christmas plans and absent friends.

***

Somewhere, in a small Parisian loft room, Lillian was spending her first Christmas abroad in the company of new friends over a bottle of red wine, whilst snow flurries swirled outside the window. Thrilled to be free of expectations and pleased to be making her way in her new life, Lillian thought how much better it would be if she could share some of it with her sister. Those gathered in the room raised a glass to a *'Joyeux Noël'* as Lillian whispered a wish towards her frosty window pane.

"Happy Christmas, Dottie."

12 GRACE

8 Rue Dauphine

Paris

23 July 1963

Dearest Dottie,

I hope you and Will are well and enjoying every moment with little Andrew. Each day I wonder what new things he will be doing. He must have grown so much. I am sure he is keeping you both very busy. Talking of busy, there has been a lot going on here so apologies for not writing sooner. I know that you will be worrying about me, but there's no need. All is going well, Sis.

I have rented an attic room – it's pretty small but has all I need. Somewhere to cook and to sleep and to sit with a book. The best part of it all is that I can see across the rooftops as I sit at my little table to eat, or to write - just like now writing this letter and watching the clouds roll by. I sit here sometimes and imagine the scenes unfolding beneath all the rooftops, the characters living and working there and that reminds me of the stories we made up when we were at Aunty Joan's farm. Do you remember them, Dottie?

I haven't found any buried treasure yet but I have started writing down my stories and thoughts whenever I can. I've quite the collection already. They make a good diary of my travels. Perhaps somebody will be interested in reading it someday? My notebooks are filling up quickly, you know me and how I always have something to say!

I wish you could see the views here, and the people. It's busy, like London, but with its own charm that I don't think I can explain well enough on paper, you just have to feel it by being here. I so love it. Each Sunday afternoon I find myself walking in the nearby gardens or along by the Seine – there is so much to see.

I'm working in the nearby corner café. My time living at the Eight Bells and working behind the bar helps but my stilted schoolgirl French leaves a lot to be desired. I am slowly picking up the language though and I have started getting to know a few of the regulars. We have clumsy conversations punctuated by lots of smiles and nods – it seems to work though.

Tonight, I'm going to dinner at Marie and Pascal's so don't have time to write too much more. They live in the flat below – friendly couple who have been very kind. Their tabby cat, Claude has taken quite a shine to me though, I think he's trying to move into my room.

Anyway, give Andrew a kiss from me. I will write again soon and next time I'll try to find a few postcards of the city, to show you some of the best views.

Love to you all,

Lil.

xx

It was two years now since Doris had received this first letter from Lillian and she had read it over and over, sometimes closing her eyes as she tried to imagine the places described in it. Since then, there had been more letters and postcards of different places in the city and beyond, as Lillian had now moved beyond the capital to explore more of France. Not wanting to discard any of them, Doris had made use of the empty toffee tin that Maggie had given them one Christmas, to keep them altogether. Each one offered a little glimpse of the new life that her sister was making and she loved it when the post dropped onto their doormat and she spied the foreign stamps, signaling another little insight into Lillian's travels.

Doris was always very disciplined about waiting to read the contents, making sure that she poured herself a cup of tea first and settled down in a moment of quiet to savour the sentences, all to herself. She knew she would read them again later to Will, when he came home from work, and usually again to Maggie whenever she next dropped by, but for the first time she read them, she always wanted that to be a moment just between the two sisters. Today she sat down with Lillian's latest postcard. This time it came from Marseille, she would have to look up where exactly that was later but for now, she devoured Lillian's words and was already starting to compose her own reply in her head.

There was so much to tell Lillian. Andrew was now toddling around and a bundle of energy. Once he could crawl he was everywhere and now that he could walk there was no stopping him. Will was working as hard as ever and remained her rock and of course had proved to be a wonderful father. The first thing he did when he got home each day was to kiss them both and to spend time playing with Andrew, or to help with the bath and bedtime routine, depending on what time he managed to get finished at work.

At the weekends, Will worked his gardening magic in the little plot that was their back yard. Although just a mundane concrete square alongside the outside toilet, Will had created interest with pots of different coloured flowers grown from cuttings or seed then nurtured through the year to bring out their best blooms. Up against the neighbours wall he had made a wooden trough from which his sweet peas grew up a trellis each year, much to Will's delight. Their little house had been updated throughout now and was a comfortable home to the three of them, soon to be four. Doris was expecting again and wished that Lillian might be able to return to spend some time with the family – for she missed her terribly.

She told Lillian how she had found another outlet for her love of music. No longer able to play piano at the pub since they had moved, she had missed the joy that gave her. Over the past six months though, she had been playing every week at a local church hall for several dance classes. Maggie would look after Andrew whilst she played, if Will had to be at work. She loved playing and also watching the graceful dancers moving in response to the simple melodies. Rows of girls in pink ballet shoes, pointing their toes and twirling around in unison. It often made her think of how she and Lillian used to dance, usually until one or both of them dissolved into a fit of giggles and could no longer keep track of the dance steps.

She finished the letter and read it back again before folding the paper and tucking it inside the envelope. Carefully she transcribed Lillian's latest address and placed the letter on the fireplace until she could get the stamps and post it. Will would be home from work soon so she set about her late afternoon routines, not knowing that Lillian would have moved on again in her travels and so never receive the letter and the invitation within it to come and visit for a while.

***

"I'll put the kettle on, Will. You both sit down while I take care of everything."

Aunty Joan had invited herself to stay for a few weeks ready to help look after Andrew and the new baby. She had arrived about a week before Doris went into labour, with home-baked treats for all and the same down to earth attitude that Doris remembered fondly from a decade ago. It was indeed a blessing to have her there, occupying Andrew or busying herself with household chores whilst Doris propped her feet up and knitted her way through the last few rows of the layette she was making.

In the last few weeks of the pregnancy, Doris had a growing feeling of unease that she could not explain. All she knew was that it did not feel this way the first time round with Andrew. Any worries she mentioned were mostly dismissed or met with advice that no two pregnancies are the same and suggestions that perhaps it was a girl this time so she might be laying differently. Doris did not know if the outcome would have been different if someone had listened to her concerns, and she guessed she would never know, but she would always carry the guilt. And her little girl, still born on the 4th September 1965, would never see the smiles of her loving parents. She had been whisked away from the hospital room as if there was nothing to see and nothing to acknowledge. Certainly staff avoided mentioning what had happened and just focused on the necessary post-natal care that Doris required, with nobody giving time to the scars that cannot be seen.

Will brought Doris home from the hospital and neither of them had any words to offer to the other. They now sat together in silence on the settee in their front room whilst Aunty Joan busied herself in the kitchen. Their whole world seemed to be unfolding in slow motion around them. The ticking from the clock amplified itself to a level far beyond that which they had ever noticed before. This room that had been such a hub of energy before, now seemed simply empty. A void.

"Supper's in the oven, a nice hearty stew. Do you both good to get some food in you," said Aunty Joan, taking charge, "so best we all have some, even you, Dot, just a little." It was clear that there was to be no arguments over this. "Little Andrew's next door with Maggie, thought that'd be for the best, just to give you a little while. He's quite happy playing in there. Now, get that tea down you while I peel the spuds."

Will and Doris had no strength to object to any of it. They sipped their tea, noticing the extra sugar that Joan had added and silent tears traced a track down Doris' cheek. Will took her hand in his and this time for once he was not the first to speak. Instead, Doris simply said

"We'll call her Grace."

13 SEPTEMBER

September changed that year from a month that Doris had previously held as one of her favourites, to one that would be synonymous with sorrow.

This September dragged, and in many ways stood still for Doris and Will. Though of course, life continued around them, with all the usual routines and events providing a pretence of normality. Yet they both felt like onlookers peering through glass at a world that they were unable to engage in.

Will had to carry on working but even the gardens that he tended could not excite him as they usually did. His work days were often solitary and for the moment, whilst he tried to make sense of what had happened and most importantly, quite how he was supposed to support Doris, being solitary in the gardens suited him. The hints of autumn's changes seeped into the trees and plants around him and the seasonal predictability proved somehow comforting.

Back home, from the armchair in their front room, Doris would watch the reddening leaves of the trees on Brewer Street as the days passed and the time came for them to start cascading on the breeze to the pavement below. Andrew played with his toys by her feet and her attention moved between him and the passers-by out of the window. Everyone going about their lives, their daily lives – business as usual, with everything continuing as normal.

"None of this is normal!" - That's what Doris wanted to scream at them, but instead she remained mostly silent.

Aunty Joan had stayed for a couple of weeks but she had to get back to the farm. Like many of her generation, she offered a perceived wisdom wrapped up in phrases that suggested Doris should forget about what had happened, focus upon the lovely son that they have and mostly not worry as they could always try again. Although such advice felt hollow, Doris knew these words were said with kind motives. At least they were better than the silences she received from others who did not offer any words, those people who crossed the street as she approached to avoid a conversation or who's talking abruptly stopped when she had found the strength to venture into a local shop. Whatever approach people took, Doris found no comfort in any of it.

For the first time since they had met, Doris found no comfort in Will either. They seemed uneasy around each other and his daily kiss as he returned from work had disappeared. With each of them trying their best not to upset the other, they found themselves limiting their talk to social necessity and their real engagement with each other was fading.

Maggie still popped in most afternoons and put the kettle on and simultaneously talked of everything and nothing. She brought cake some days and played with Andrew, sitting herself on the floor to chat away as he played. And as she did, Doris slowly began to focus on what was happening around her and to join in with parts of her conversation.

It was on one of these afternoons, at the end of September, when Maggie suddenly stopped twirling her long, black hair and stood up from the front room carpet to ask Doris a question.

"When's the last time you and Will went out somewhere?" asked Maggie. She stood with her head cocked slightly to one side, for once silently awaiting a response.

"Um, I'm not sure, Maggie." Doris struggled to remember a specific occasion but knew it must have been before they had Andrew and offered a non-committal response along those lines. She thought of various moments in time when they had been just a couple and not a little family unit. A walk holding hands in a park, a drink at the local pub, an evening at the cinema, nothing grand or elaborate, just the sort of things that all young couples do. She switched her mind from such memories to tune in to what Maggie was saying.

"That's all sorted then, this Friday will do. I'll help to spruce you up in the afternoon, we'll fix your hair and all. Then Mam and I will babysit, so you and Will can go out for the evening."

"Oh, I don't know, Maggie," Doris tried to remonstrate. "I doubt Will is ready for that either."

"Sure he is, Fred's telling him the plan today. He's going to meet him after work, see how he is and explain." Maggie's mischievous eyes danced as she continued, particularly when she revealed how Fred was complicit in the planning.

"You're quite a force to be reckoned with sometimes, Maggie. When you've put your mind to it."

"Exactly, just like me Mam says. Now, what do you say?"

"Um, I don't know."

"Ah, come on, it'll be fine."

"But, Maggie…"

"You know we won't take no for an answer."

"I can see that," conceeded Doris while a hint of a smile began forming "and with Fred muscling in on it too, I guess we've no choice."

"That's the spirit, Friday it is then."

"So it seems."

"Now, shall we have another cup of tea?"

With that, the subject was closed and Maggie retreated to the kitchen to boil the kettle and warm the teapot, pleased with herself to be doing something constructive to help her friends.

***

It was cold that Friday night, the sort of crisp cold that confirms that summer evenings have long gone and autumn has flung open its door. Doris and Will were making ready to walk home from their evening out. They had eaten a simple meal of ham, egg and chips at a café a few streets away, sat together at a table by the window where the distraction of the street scene might fill the gaps in conversation. Though there had been many of those as they first sat down and ordered their food, both worked hard to rectify that and gradually found themselves relaxing into a closer version of what they had always been before. Will spoke a little of his gardening schedule at work, Doris talked of how scheming Maggie and Fred had been and Will commented on how beautiful Doris looked.

An hour or so passed and the café saw a steady stream of locals, eager to escape the night for a while, cocooned in the warmth of familiarity and an honest square meal. By now the windows had steamed over and they were both somewhat reluctant to leave their cosy corner spot. Will slurped the last of his mug of strong tea and exchanged smiles with Doris as they both stood to put on their coats, ready to brave the walk home.

Outside the café, the blast of cold air forced Will to turn up his coat collar and Doris to sink her hands into her pockets.

"Blimey, it's a bit brass monkeys tonight," gasped Will, watching his white breath on the night air and rubbing his hands together.

"It is that," Doris replied. "Won't take us long to get home though, and put the kettle on."

Their brisk walk took them along the High Street and past the church at pace but as they turned the corner into the top of Brewer Street, Doris paused to look up at the night sky. It was an unusually clear night.

"Look at the stars, Will. They're all out tonight."

"Worth the cold for that view. All looking down on us."

"And Grace is up there too."

Doris felt Will's hands rest on her shoulders and she moved her gaze from the stars and into his hazel eyes, those kind hazel eyes.

"It will be okay, Doris. She'll always be part of us."

He gently kissed her lips and moved his hands to hold her around the waist and Doris sank into the hug, letting his words and his arms protect her. It felt like a long time as they stood in that embrace, feeling the warmth and acceptance of each other, drawing strength from each other's understanding. Then, without further words, they broke their embrace to hold hands and walk down the road to number 53.

UNRAVELLING

LOSING TRACK

(2015)

14 IN THE GARDEN

Doris was not in her usual spot in the garden room when Lucy arrived at Green Meadows this week. Lucy had breezed past the reception desk after signing her name, without engaging in conversation. If she had waited a few minutes, she would have been told that Doris was still in her bedroom and that she had not managed to eat much of her lunch. This information was now being shared with her by the duty nurse, Louise, who had asked Lucy to take a seat in her office for a moment. She had been too caught up in her own thoughts of phrases from last night's conversation with her father, phrases which were now echoing in her mind as Lucy cast her eyes around the little office room.

The room had a lot crammed into its small square space. On one wall, a shelf was full with assorted A4 binders, bulky manuals of correct procedures for social care, medical text books and an in-tray that was struggling to contain its overflowing paperwork. Lucy's concentration wandered, assaulted by the whirring extractor fan, last night's recurring scene and fragments of what Louise was saying, all tossing around her head to compete for her attention. Instead she steadied her focus upon the chart which was drawn out on the whiteboard opposite her.

The board displayed all the information required in the running of Green Meadows each week. It was possible to see at a glance which staff were working each day, which residents they were overseeing and which of them needed specific medications or treatment actions at different times of the day. Lucy recognised the necessity of such rotas and routines for the home to operate efficiently but it was such uniformity that Doris usually objected to, struggling as she did now to understand the routines of daily life.

Lucy realised that her gaze was following her Gran's line on the whiteboard chart and at once felt the inner glow of self-consciousness rising, compelling her to stop staring at it. She returned her focus to Louise's brown eyes as they peered at her over half-frame glasses. Louise was the epitome of efficiency, her hair simply fixed back with a small tortoiseshell barrette and her uniform neatly pressed. She had Doris' file open on the desk, full of charts and typed up notes but she closed it when she saw the anxiety apparent on Lucy's face.

"There's nothing to worry about, I just wanted to catch you before you go up to Doris today."

"Thank you," Lucy replied. "Dad told me about the phone call last night. He said that Gran's getting more confused."

Louise smiled back and thought better of continuing the conversation within the clinical environment of the office.

"Shall I walk with you up to your Gran's room? We can talk on the way, save wasting your visitor time."

Louise ushered Lucy out of the office and up the central staircase. This was one feature of the original house that had not been lost to the clumsiness of conversion and the sweeping curve of its wooden balustrade sat strangely at odds in its elegance. On the way to the first floor, Lucy listened as Louise explained that her Gran had just had a run of days where she seemed to be more unsettled, more confused.

"It's quite typical in dementia patients, Lucy, much to be expected."

"I see."

"We've been working on activities to help with memory, making connections that she can talk about."

"She does like to talk about the past, even if it all gets muddled up."

"Yes. That doesn't matter really, it all helps – the familiarity."

They were outside Gran's bedroom now and Louise paused with her hand on the door handle. Giving Lucy another smile, she added "She's had her coat on all morning. She thinks she's going out with her husband later."

"Granddad Will, oh dear. She keeps forgetting," Lucy adjusted her bag on her shoulder. "Would it be okay if I took her out in the garden?"

"I think that's a great idea. A change of scene might be nice."

"Yes, hopefully."

"I'll ask Sam to pop out a tea tray once you've settled out there, just call if you need any help."

Louise opened Gran's bedroom door for Lucy to go in.

"Doris, we have a visitor for you," said Louise. "Your lovely Lucy's here to see you."

Doris was walking back and forth the few steps distance it took to repeatedly pass the bay window in her room. She was clearly agitated but paused when she saw Lucy move closer and waited to hear her speak.

"It's Tuesday, Gran, my usual visit day. Shall we go out in the garden?"

The suggestion seemed to take Doris off guard and she stopped her pacing and pulled her coat closer across her chest.

"I see you've got your coat on ready," Lucy added, attempting to cajole Doris into action.

Doris returned her granddaughter's smile and allowed her to link their arms together. They made slow progress over to her walking frame in the corner of her room, passing the dressing table where a few of Gran's belongings hinted echoes of distant times. There was her hair brush, scent bottle, a pot of moisturising cream and her powder compact, all brought to Green Meadows from her bedroom at home, in the hope of making her feel the comfort of their familiarity.

Beyond those items were a couple of family photographs stood at each end of the dressing table. One appeared to have been taken on a holiday in the seventies, and Lucy guessed that her father looked about nine or ten years old in it. On the other corner of the dressing table was another photo frame which contained more recent family shots. Lucy and her brothers were there, as well as pictures of her cousins. It was doubtful whether Doris would be able to name any of them now. They left the smiling faces behind and made their way along the corridor to take the lift down towards the garden.

Louise and Sam nodded in their direction as Lucy helped Doris out into the gardens at the rear of Green Meadows. Lucy was immediately grateful for the fresh air hitting her face and paused to take in the view before them. There was a sweeping lawn with a smooth, wide pathway that formed a loop around its edges, making access easy for those residents with additional walking aids or wheelchairs. Alongside the pathway were mature shrubs and a few trees, some holding bird feeders, another a sun catcher, both of these additions designed to provide the residents with areas of interest to focus on.

Nearer the house, a gravel area with a few pots dotted around, displayed bedding plants, chosen for their colour and easy maintenance. In one corner of this area, the staff and a few residents who were able to manage it, had worked with a local charity to build a raised bed and stock it with vegetables. The project gave some of the residents the opportunity to do a little gardening, something which many of them missed from their home lives. Lucy looked at the vegetable plot and thought how much her granddad would have enjoyed looking after it.

She helped Doris to steady her frame on the garden path and then the two of them strolled onwards, slowly completing a lap of the lawn, past the azaleas and rhododendrons in the far corner. They were all in bud and would soon be adding bursts of pink and purple hues to the garden. Nearby, in the shade of a couple of trees, a few early bluebells were dancing in the breeze, a sight which reminded Lucy that she had the scarf in her bag.

"Oh, I've just remembered, Gran. I've got something for you."

Doris looked interested to find out what it might be as Lucy helped her to sit at one of the little tables on the gravel area. Sam headed over with a tea tray at that point and offered to bring out a blanket for Gran, as although it was a sunny day she might feel too chilly if they sat there for a while.

Lucy plopped two sugar cubes into Gran's tea and stirred it for her. She explained how she had come across the scarf among some old boxes of Gran's things.

"I thought you might like to have it again. I think the colour is just beautiful."

Doris smiled as Lucy helped her to put it on, tying it loosely under her chin to wear like a headscarf.

"Thank you dear, did Lillian send it?"

Perhaps Lillian did originally, or perhaps Doris had worn it sometime when she was out with Lillian. Lucy thought it best to find Gran a reassuring answer.

"Yes, Gran. I think she did. Isn't that lovely?"

"Lovely, yes. Lovely Lillian. She tells stories, you know," Doris pulled at the scarf bow tied loosely under her chin. "Where are we going dear?"

"Shall we just have a cup of tea, for now?" Lucy asked.

"Tea and two sugars, please Lillian."

"Yes, that's right. All ready for you."

Lucy slid the teacup towards her Gran making no attempt to correct her mistake. She wondered what had happened for the sisters to have lost touch over the years and what had become of Lillian. She decided she would return to the stack of letters and postcards in the tin when she got home. Lucy sipped her tea and was pleased to see that her Gran now seemed calm, sat in the garden with the scarf framing her face. There would be no drawing today, she was just happy to sit with her Gran and let the time tick over.

15 TRAIN RIDES

Lucy picked her way through the swelling commuter crowd to take up her position on the platform and wait for the next train home. She usually managed to get a seat for at least part of the journey but this looked unlikely today. Arriving later than usual she faced being crammed into the carriage between armpits and newspapers, to centre her body weight with the swaying motion of the journey in an attempt to remain upright. An unsavoury prospect.

From her spot, a few metres along from the illuminated arrivals sign, she could see that she had three minutes before her train was due and took the opportunity to send a brief text to her father. This was not something she usually did but after their chat last night she thought she would let him know how this afternoon's visit had gone.

Hi Dad.

Gran ok after a while but v confused at 1ˢᵗ.

Tell more when I'm home, L x

Lucy reflected on all that had happened at Green Meadows today and how the change to their little routine had unsettled her. With that in mind, she considered how hard it must be for her Gran regularly coping with uncertainties, trapped within a mind and body that no longer wanted to cooperate with her. Resentful as she might feel to have this minor disruption in their Tuesday routine, Lucy checked herself for entertaining such thoughts.

The train arrived and Lucy jostled her way forward with the throng of commuters to take up a spot inside the train, leaning her left side against the glass partition between the doors and the row of seats at one end of the carriage. Hemmed in by other passengers, most of whom were taller than her, she looked down to avoid making eye contact and hoped the journey would not take too long.

She had not received a reply to her text and would not be able to check her phone now anyway. Usually when travelling on the train, she would spend her time reading one of her books or failing that, her attention would phase in and out on the adverts and notices displayed around the carriage. She habitually found herself reading and re-reading them, scanning over the order of stops on the line, the merits of a private medical insurance scheme or in joining a recruitment agency to secure the perfectly tailored job. Sometimes there would be an advert with a picture of a holiday destination and she would imagine herself jetting off to be there, feeling an inner calm as she watched the sun go down.

Calm was what had been missing from today's visit, well at least it had taken most of the afternoon before she felt that Gran was calmer. Just before Lucy left, Gran had been able to talk a little. A few fragments about colourful flowers... a day out, holding Will's hand... some stars in the sky. Some of the strands made no sense at all but Lucy gleaned that there had been a special day, sometime in the past, when Will and Doris had walked around gardens and they had both been dressed up. There were prizes and lots of people and wherever it was, Doris was proud and Will's smile had beamed back at her. Lucy would like to have stayed longer with Gran, to have heard more about this day and to have sketched a little of the garden at Green Meadows but perhaps there would be time for that next week.

A few more stops along the line and Lucy would be off the train and walking up the road to home. She hoped dinner would be something comforting and that her father would be home and ready to talk like he had last night.

***

Andrew had taken his after-dinner coffee into his little workspace tonight and asked Lucy if she wanted to join him. The space was little more than a corner of the dining room that had been sectioned off to make room for a desk, a lamp and a little filing cabinet adorned by a single, variegated-leafed, pot plant. He rarely did any work there, but it was an option if he needed it and a space to house all the usual important family documents, tucked away within the drawers of the filing cabinet.

He could not have worked in there this evening though, for alongside his desk there were several boxes from the house clearance stacked up, awaiting decisions on their fate. Andrew ran his finger along the top of one of them.

"My train set, Lucy. I guess we should sell it, nobody's going to play with it now."

"You don't have to Dad. If it's important to you. I wondered if it was yours, when I saw it in the attic."

"Oh yes, Lucy. It's mine. Spent a lot of time playing with it, when I was a boy."

"That's nice."

"Still I can't hang on to everything."

As the two of them sorted through some of the boxes that evening, Andrew talked of his memories playing with his train set and times when his parents had bought him a new engine or carriage for it. He could remember spending hours setting up the track and running the trains back and forth along it. The more he spoke the more he became convinced that Lucy might be right and that he should store the train set away, at least for a while.

As he talked of tracks and train rides, Lucy was reminded of a day out at a steam railway when she was little. The memory was a little sketchy. Had it just been her and her grandparents? She could not remember her parents being there which she thought was strange, now that she was discovering quite how much interest her father had in trains. There had been quite a lot of days out with just her grandparents though, days when her parents were both at work. This must have been one of those days.

Lucy recalled an image of the three of them cupping their hands around hot chocolates as they stood on the station platform, waiting for their train to arrive and then watching all the doors swing open and everybody bustling about. There was noise and steam and colour. A whistle, a flag waving, an excitement as she was lifted by two strong arms over the gap between the platform edge and the train. She had always felt safe with her grandparents. Protected. Lately she had noticed a compulsion to protect her father. Stood by his train set, peering into the box, he looked strangely vulnerable.

"I think you should keep it, Dad."

"Maybe."

"I think Gran would like that."

"Mum, might not," he joked. "But I'll find somewhere for it."

"Shall I get you another coffee, Dad?" Lucy asked as she picked up both of their cups from the little desk.

"Yes please, Lucy." Andrew picked up another box. "Um, do you want to come with me to see Gran next weekend? We can catch the train together after lunch?"

"Okay, Dad. I'd like that."

She went in search of a couple of her Dad's favourite biscuits to go with this coffee, mulling over their conversations. His suggestion had surprised Lucy but he had obviously been concerned by what she had told him about the afternoon's visit - the talk in the nursing office, the walk around the garden and Gran's confusion. She realised that neither of them had really talked about such things before and she wondered why. Maybe they were both doing the same thing, pretending that it was not really happening for as long as they could manage not having to talk about it. Sadly, that could not stay the case for much longer.

16 MISSING THOUGHTS

"I don't want that, that... stuff."

Doris found it increasingly difficult to remember the names of objects that had hitherto been familiar to her. Today she had lost the words for the food on her plate.

"It's mashed potato, Doris. You've eaten it before," said Sam, patiently labelling his way around her dinner plate as he encouraged her to eat a little of its contents. "Mashed potato, carrots and minced beef. Like a cottage pie, very nice."

"Like a cottage..."

Her sentence hung midway in the air and she ate a forkful before continuing, this time singing part of a lyric that had entered her head and distracted her away from the current battle in the dining room. "In a cottage in the wood, a little old man at the window stood..."

Sam let her sing a little, between forkfuls, as it seemed to soothe her.

"Saw a rabbit running by..."

"Just a bit more, now," coaxed Sam between the lines of her song.

It was strange how song lyrics came more readily to Doris than everyday vocabulary. Lately, she had been getting more easily distracted and the more she found that words were failing her, the more aggravated she could become. Sam tried to strike a balance between letting Doris fumble around for the words that she wanted and stepping in to help out to avoid her becoming distressed. Having worked in the care sector for many years now, he was good at his job and always mindful not to speak for the residents, quick to point out that each one was still their own person. They may no longer have the best grip on reality but he worked hard to support them in still having a voice. That was important to Sam and even on the most challenging days, he could be relied upon to find a smile and a good word to say to lift everyone's spirits.

Sam had noticed how Doris loved her singing. Some afternoons if Doris was sitting in the garden room after lunch, he would select some music to play to see if it brought a smile to her face. She was not the only resident to appreciate this gesture and though many could not recall the lyrics, it was noticeable how many of them could suddenly look more relaxed as music spread its spell around the room.

"Shall we play some tunes this afternoon, Doris?"

Doris smiled and gently moved her fingers up and down on the edge of the table. If there had been a piano at Green Meadows, it would have been interesting to see if she could still play a tune or two of her own. Tunes from when Daisy sat dozing by the fireside, or when rows of girls stretched and swirled in unison. It may well have been the case. After all, some skills learnt as a child can remain resilient to the damage dementia inflicts elsewhere to the mind and body, for a while at least.

Either way, that was the afternoon sorted. Following the cottage pie dinner and a pudding of jam roly poly and custard, Doris and most of her fellow residents found themselves a spot in either the garden room or the television lounge. Doris felt calmer after eating and even better once Sam had set his playlist going, a nostalgic playlist designed to appeal to the residents. As she sat in her usual spot, she wondered when her smiling visitor would return, the girl who draws.

It felt like a while since she had last been but Doris could not be sure. She vaguely remembered the last time she had come, the visit felt different. Someone else was with her and Doris was sure she should have known him.

***

A while before supper, Doris sat at the foot of her bed lost in the maze of her mind. She was trying hard to hold onto a single thought, any thought would do but each time she tried to grasp one to follow, it flew just out of reach like a feather on a breeze. Some days, names would stick around but mostly not. An image of a face, a place or a moment in time would blur in and out of focus and Doris could not make sense of it.

She looked around her room and knew that most of the objects there belonged to her, though she may not recall where they had come from. Her gaze fell upon the small, silver photo frame on the dressing table. Its oval shape outlining an image of a family scene, a family of three, stood by a harbour wall on a sunny day. She picked up the frame and held it carefully, staring into the picture in an attempt to will the scene into life, to kick start its memories.

The photograph had been taken on a Devon holiday in 1972. The day had been hot and Andrew and Will had spent several hours crabbing, perched on the stone steps of the harbour wall, dangling simple crabbing lines into the water as they persevered to retrieve any lucky catch for their buckets which sat alongside them. Doris had a good view of their activity from the bench she occupied and watched happily, between the pages of the book she was reading, as the afternoon passed by. The intermittent calls of curious seagulls punctuated the air but otherwise the noises of the small harbour town provided a soft backdrop to the scene. There was the slow chug of a passing fishing boat or the half-heard phrase of a conversation drifting by as other tourists enjoyed the peace of the place.

When the interest in crabbing had waned and the catch returned to the sea, the three of them walked the length of the harbour wall to a little ice-cream parlour where a few tables and chairs dotted the promenade, beneath red and white striped parasols erected to offer customers a little shade. They found a space to sit and each devoured the delights of a Knickerbocker glory.

Their week away had been full of simple treats and many outdoor adventures that a nine-year-old boy would revel in. The days were full of long walks and picnics, beach days of swimming and rock-pooling, visits to sites of smuggling tales and medieval battles. The evenings spent in a pub garden where Andrew sucked on the stripy straw in his bottle of Coca-Cola and shook the salt into his packet of crisps, or for a special treat the three of them ate scampi and chips in a basket, listening to the sounds of the resident band coming from the dancefloor inside. After such days and evenings, they would then leave the lights of the promenade behind them to walk back along the cliff path with only the soundtrack of the waves below and torchlight to find their caravan.

All of these memories were there waiting for Doris, if she could only have stepped back into the scenes and navigated her way to find her little family. Instead, her frustration grew and she cast the photograph aside, throwing it against her pillows. She wanted to run, she wanted to dance, in reality she could not work out what she wanted for most of the time.

Feeling agitated, she managed to direct her walking frame along the corridor and headed determinedly for the lift. She was going to go out for the evening, if she could just get past the busy-body staff who watched her and make it out of the front door.

CELEBRATIONS

(1975)

17 A NIGHT ON THE TOWN

Saturday mornings were always busy and today was no exception. Will had left the house early with Andrew to watch him play football with his school team at the local park, a father – son ritual that they both enjoyed. Doris made her way to the church hall for a nine o'clock start, playing piano for several dance classes before lunch. As usual it was after midday when they got back home and each grabbed something quick for lunch before settling into their chosen afternoon pursuit, grateful for a spot of relaxation.

Will divided his time between watching sport on the television and pottering a little in the back yard, pruning and tending the plants in the various pots he had collected over the years. Some weeks Doris would join Will in the back yard but today she thumbed her way through a magazine, indulging in the calm of the house before it would be time to prepare the evening meal. Andrew was happy to retreat to his room and immerse himself in his own world, with his Lego or comic books.

All three of them were happy, engaged in their Saturday pursuits when the doorbell rang, a little after three o'clock. Doris left her magazine on the sideboard as she went to answer the front door. A moment later and her shriek shattered the peace in the house. Andrew and Will came running to join her to discover that Lillian was standing on the doorstep with a small suitcase in her hand.

"Surprise!" beamed Lillian.

If Lillian had meant to utter anything more, it was unintelligible as she and Doris flung their arms around each other and clung on, crying happy tears together. Will retrieved the suitcase from the doorstep and was the first to speak.

"Just look at the pair of you, how lovely to see you, Lil."

Andrew looked on dumbfounded and more than a little concerned until Will explained that Lillian was the travelling aunty that his mother often talked about.

"Oh my," Lillian chipped in, breaking free from the emotional embrace and stepping into the front room. "That can't be my little nephew."

"Well, it's been a while, Lil." Doris closed the door and ushered Lillian to sit down. "I can't believe you're here. And you look so well."

Andrew perched himself on the arm of the settee, curious to know more about this lady with the beaming smile. He listened to her animated conversation of travel and oversees jobs and a journey made so that she could spend a few days with the family. Lillian paused at that point to ask about staying.

"If it's okay with you, for me to stay for a few nights? I can always look for a hotel room, if I'm in the way?"

There was to be no debate on this issue. Of course Lillian would stay and it would be like old times, times that they all started discussing whilst Andrew was dispatched to the kitchen to brew a pot of tea. As they chatted, Lillian began taking gifts for each of them out of her suitcase. Duty free whisky for Will, some sweets for Andrew and a small giftwrapped box for Doris, which Lillian was eager for her to open.

"I hope you like it, Dottie. It's from Venice," Lillian explained, leaning in to watch Doris' reaction as she took the delicate brooch out of its box.

"It's beautiful, Lil. I love it, how thoughtful," she smiled and carefully turned the brooch over several times in her hand. "I didn't know you'd been to Venice."

"Oh yes, I had a few days holiday there with my friend, Judith, but I can tell you more about that later. Put it on." Lillian's enthusiasm made Doris smile.

"It looks expensive, I think I should keep it for a special occasion."

"Nonsense," declared Lillian. "Wear it tonight!"

"What, whilst I do the dishes?" Doris teased but Lillian was quick to reply.

"No, if it's okay with Will and Andrew, I thought I'd steal you away this evening and treat you to a night on the town. Is that alright, Will? A bit of time, just two sisters together?"

Will was not going to argue with that and straight away reassured Doris that he would fix supper for him and Andrew and that she and Lillian should go and have a lovely time. The rest of the plans were made as they drank their tea and Andrew tucked into his box of sweets.

***

Doris and Lillian caught the number 15 bus from the stop at the Town Hall, not far from Brewer Street. With the added bonus of securing the front seats on the top deck, they had a view of the bustle of London as they passed by a kaleidoscope of colour and lights illuminating the night scene that was coming to life around them. The larger stores with their window displays lit up, a newspaper seller calling attention to his pile of Evening Standards, bars and cafes welcoming a steady stream of customers and then, as the bus reached The Strand, lights proudly announcing the different shows taking place within each of the theatres, enticing their audiences inside.

Doris was excited to be amongst such busy scenes, the little aspects of city life that unfolded every night of the week. But tonight she was there to see them, instead of quietly playing out her usual domestic family routines. Tonight she was dressed up and glowing, inside and out and best of all, she had her sister by her side. They got off the bus near Trafalgar Square and made their way across it to find somewhere to eat, pausing a while by the fountains to soak up the atmosphere.

"Have you missed all this, Lillian?" Doris asked as she looked in her purse for a couple of coins.

"I've missed you more," Lillian replied. "Every city is different but they're all only as good as the people who are in them."

"I've missed you too, so much. Have they been good to you?" she asked.

"Who?"

"The people in your cities?"

"Oh yes, I've been very lucky."

"Maybe, but it's down to you too. People like being around you."

"I don't know about that but perhaps we do make our own luck."

"Well, just in case yours runs out, here, take this and make a wish, Lil," said Doris, passing Lillian a penny. "Make it a good one."

Doris motioned for Lillian to throw her penny into the fountain. As they each closed their eyes for a moment and tossed their coins into the cool water, they looked more like the girls of their youth than the two women in their thirties that they actually were. Stood there in their floral print dresses, thoughts of childhood games and teenage dreams would be easy to conjure up but there was much more to be said than that. More than could be conveyed in the letters sent between them, details that could help to join up the dots.

They found a little bistro café in a side street near the square and Lillian insisted that Doris order whatever she wanted from the menu. She had some spare money from her latest publishing advance and was determined to treat her sister. Doris hesitated as she looked through the menu and soon asked Lillian to order for the both of them. She appeared much more at ease in their surroundings and flashed a confident smile at the waiter as he went off to retrieve their bottle of Mateus Rosé.

"Quite the find, this place. Reminds me of Paris," said Lillian, nodding at a few of the couples sat at nearby tables.

"Does it?" asked Doris. "I tried to imagine it all, from your letters."

Doris sat back in her chair and nibbled on a bread roll, fixing her eyes on Lillian whose travelling tales began to take full flow. Listening to her sister, she was at once transported back to the days when Lillian always had a story to tell. It was no surprise that she had been able to turn this skill into a writing career. The fact that this career was taking her to so many different places was quite remarkable though, twelve years on from that first train to Paris.

As the evening went on they shared snippets of their lives between mouthfuls of good food. Lillian talked of places she had been, people she had met and the plans that she had yet to fulfil. It all sounded full of excitement and adventure, aspects that Doris remembered her craving as they were growing up but there was one thing that Lillian was missing in all of this. Family.

Doris spoke of her family life, and although her tales were far less exotic in content, Lillian was just as keen to listen to them. She wanted to hear about Andrew's school days and Will's work, how often Doris played piano now and the last holiday that the three of them had taken. Each sister was keen to share moments from their differing experiences but beyond that, they were mostly content with just being in each other's company.

Lillian moved the last flakes of her Dover sole around the plate and took advantage of a lull in the conversation to confront something she had been struggling with. "I'm sorry, Dottie."

"What for?"

"That I wasn't here when you needed me most, when you lost..."

Lillian broke off midway through her sentence and cast her eyes down towards the fork that she was twiddling. She felt Doris take her hand across the little bistro table.

"Grace?"

"Yes, Grace. I should have been there."

"It's alright, Lil. It's a long time ago now"

"I needed to say it though."

"I know. Thank you."

Lillian looked at the brave sister in front of her and squeezed her hand.

"Now, Lil," Doris continued. "Have we got time for pudding?"

Lillian's smile returned and she was quick to reply, "There's always time for pudding."

She waved towards the waiter to summon a dessert menu.

"How long are you staying, Lil?"

"I was thinking a week. I've got a few bits to sort out because, well, I was going to wait to tell all three of you together but…"

"What is it? You can't leave me in suspense now." Doris smiled and waited for Lillian's response. Lillian took a moment for an intake of breath.

"I'm moving to Canada."

18 BIRTHDAY TREATS

It was pouring with rain. The sort of heavy deluge that April often likes to dot amongst its sunnier skies and sends torrents streaming down the streets. But nothing was going to dampen their spirits this afternoon. Doris and Will sat in a pair of red, moulded plastic seats across the table from Andrew and his school friend, Paul, as they tucked into their burgers and chips in the Wimpy bar. Andrew had been allowed to choose one friend for this birthday treat of a meal out and a cinema trip to see Star Wars, the film of the year – as far as Andrew was concerned anyway.

"Leave some for the rest of us, love," joked Doris, reminding Andrew not to squeeze out the entire contents of the tomato shaped ketchup dispenser on his plate.

"Alright, Mum."

She wondered how much teenage boys could eat if given the chance and smiled at Will as the boys chatted away and tucked into the last of their chips whilst ordering themselves a brown derby dessert each. An indulgent mixture of hot doughnuts and a melting flourish of Mr Whippy ice-cream swirled upon them, sprinkled with nuts and chocolate sauce. Andrew and Paul's eyes widened when these arrived but they somehow found the space to eat them.

Will and Doris did not bother with dessert and had a coffee instead, but they were pleased to see the boys relishing their treats. Now that Will was doing well with his gardening business and Doris had been working part-time again, they could afford a few treats and days out from time to time. This was as good a time as any for a treat - celebrating Andrew's fifteenth birthday, they were both feeling proud of the young man he had become. She thought back to when she was fifteen. It was hard to recall many details but she worked out it was the year that she and Lillian had stayed on the farm with Aunty Joan. How different times were then. So much that they took for granted now, was unheard of or scarce at the time, yet there was still fun to be had if you tried. Of course she had always had her sister around to make mischief with. Andrew never had a sibling to play with, to plot and plan with. Doris would always regret that.

She thought about the last time she had seen Lillian, before her move so far away. There had been a lot to process during that visit. Feelings of excitement for her sister to be off to a new job in a new country and sadness to be losing her again, as both of them returned to their separate lives. Three years on and Lillian was doing well, making her new life in Canada, according to the letters that still came through the letter box from time to time. She was renting a little home in Montreal with Judith – the friend who had helped her to secure the job there. Lillian appeared to be loving the country and all the opportunities it gave her.

"Eat up, boys. Film's starting in half an hour,"

Will's voice cut into Doris' thoughts, bringing her focus back to the Wimpy bar and she watched him go up to the counter to pay the bill. It was only a short walk to the ABC Cinema on Mile End Road but they were grateful that the rain appeared to be easing off. There should be time enough to get their tickets for the two o'clock screening. Now that the film had been showing for weeks, there would be no problem getting in. It might not be her first choice to see but she had to admit she was excited to be spending the afternoon that way. Years back, she and Will would have spent Saturday evenings holding hands at the pictures but that seemed a long time ago and she couldn't recall the last film they had seen.

"Can me and Paul sit near the front, Mum?" asked Andrew, clearly preferring to put a little distance between himself and his parents as they made their way down the aisle to choose from the empty seats dotted around the auditorium.

"Course you can, love, we'll meet you outside after."

She walked off with Will to find a couple of seats further back. This is how it was going to be from now on, she thought. Their world had revolved around Andrew, with him feeling even more precious once it was obvious there would be no further children. After losing Grace all that time ago, there had been a couple of times when a skipped period gave hope of a further pregnancy but nothing materialised from it and she and Will grew to accept that their family was complete with the three of them.

Andrew was a bright boy and was destined to do well in his exams next year. He hoped to go to the local college and seemed determined to work hard to get there. Though lately, there were more times when his homework was pushed aside in favour of spending time out with his mates. Doris did not object to that though, she took comfort from knowing he had good friends and that he was having a little fun. She had always been keen that he should have lots of opportunities to mix with other children, to avoid all his time being around adults.

She thought about the modest fuss they had made of him that morning, with a few balloons hung up and smiles all round as he opened his gifts. After the film they would be lighting candles on the simple cake that she had made for Andrew, a chocolate sponge on his request, as it had always been his favourite. Then she guessed that he and Paul would disappear up to his room for the rest of the evening. Simple birthday treats, some might think, but treats all the same.

The main lights faded and the projectionist started the run of adverts for the local businesses. Doris folded her coat onto the empty chair next to her and began to take in the scene around her, the sounds, the excitement, the big screen, the afternoon out with her husband next to her and her son making his way into his fifteenth year and the independence of his future beyond. Everything changes and there always seems to be a surprise or two, good or bad, waiting for you around the corner. The best that Doris had learnt to do over time was to make the most of the time she was in and to know that there always seemed to be somebody around who would help out when she needed it.

"You, alright, Dot?" Will asked.

"Yes. Happy isn't he?"

"Having a great time, I'd say."

"We did alright."

"We did indeed. Now, time to see what all the fuss is about, film's starting."

She took hold of Will's hand and sat back in her chair, ready to enjoy the film as the opening of the story crawled up the screen.

19 THE HAT BOX

Doris had the house to herself. It was the Wednesday after Andrew's birthday celebrations. She had put a beef casserole in the oven that morning and picked up a fresh bloomer loaf from the baker's, along with a few other bits of shopping from the little cluster of local shops a few streets away. This meant that she had no further dinner preparations to concern herself with, other than slicing a little bread to accompany the casserole when she served it up later. With other household chores done too, she was left with a few hours to spare until Andrew would be home from school.

Doris didn't work on Wednesdays and usually filled her time off with cleaning and the jobs that piled up whilst she was out at her part-time office job but today she had decided to use her time to have a good sort out, as she liked to call it. So far in her quest, she had managed to stack a few piles of clothes on her bed and begun to fill a couple of cardboard boxes that she had brought home from the office, with some of Andrew's old toys. She was working out which items to donate to the next jumble sale at the local church hall and which ones she felt a stronger connection with. For those in the second category, Doris was determined to find a way to store them in the attic by jostling what limited space remained there.

Between the furniture and all the items that she was sorting, there was not much space left in the bedroom for Doris to move around. Their double bed sat between two MFI bedside wardrobes with a connecting overhead cupboard. A matching chest of drawers and an ottoman where bedding was stored took up the wall space at the foot of the bed. There was a window framed with brown curtains on one wall and on the opposite wall a round, yellow, plastic framed mirror broke up the floral wallpaper and hung between the bedroom door and the hatch to the attic.

Doris turned on the radio that sat upon their chest of drawers and started to sing along, "Night fever, we know how to show it…" In buoyant mood she opened the little hatch door and pulled an old suitcase and a hat box out from the nearest part of the attic. She placed them onto the beige continental quilt which covered their bed.

Doris had never been one to hold on to lots of possessions and mostly kept things only for necessity – clothes and household objects were well used and only got replaced when they no longer functioned. Occasionally though, she would keep hold of something out of sentimentality. A well-used favourite toy or book, a special piece of jewellery or an accessory that conjured up happy memories and was seen as too precious to give away, such items usually made it into the attic eventually.

She began to put a few clothes from the bed into the suitcase but her attention kept returning to the hat box. It did not take long for Doris to give into her curiosity and she made herself a space on the bed to slide off the lid of the hat box and look inside. Nestled safely inside, within a wrap of tissue paper, was the turquoise hat that she had worn for Fred and Maggie's wedding. She missed the days when

Maggie regularly popped in from next door and without thinking, Doris had put it on and moved over to the bedroom mirror to adjust the hat accordingly as she smiled back at her reflection.

Doris remembered doing the same thing on the wedding morning, a sunny, spring morning in 1969. With thoughts of that happy day in her mind, she started dancing round the room. It had been a simple affair at the nearby registry office, with just a few witnesses present, but they had all dressed up for the day. Will, in his suit, with Doris on his arm, telling her that she looked like a film star, before they went off to wish his older brother and their effervescent neighbour all the luck in the world. She loved how her hat complimented her simple shift dress that day. Even now, looking back at the smooth pill box shape with its delicate net covering dotting across her forehead, she grew taller with the air of elegance it gave her. Perhaps that was why she had kept it, after all she could not envisage another time when she would make use of it again.

She was never quite sure when Fred and Maggie had realised that they had something more than a friendship, certainly they had known each other a fair while before anything more had blossomed between them. That was how it appeared to her and Will anyway. Maggie had become almost a substitute sister to Doris in Lillian's absence and so was usually around whenever Fred dropped by to see them and as time went on, she seemed to make more of a point of being so. To this day, Doris was unsure if the marriage had been one based on romance or a more platonic need for companionship but either way, they both seemed to be very happy.

Both being in their thirties when they married, and Fred nearing forty, neither of them wanted a big or outlandish wedding, preferring instead to keep their money for a trip to Ireland by way of a honeymoon. In reality, it was so Fred could meet Maggie's many relatives and she could show off all that her village and the surrounding area had to offer. Maggie hoped it all lived up to the teenage memories that she had of it and either way she could not contain her excitement about the trip, talking as much about that as she did the preparations for the wedding. Then again, Maggie could talk about anything.

"Are you up there, Dot?" Will's voice gave Doris a start as he called out to her. He didn't usually get home from work until later.

"Yes," she replied. "I'm just putting some stuff in the attic. Is everything okay?"

Doris put the hat back in the box and closed the clasps on the suitcase as she heard the tread of his footsteps on the stairs.

"Oh yeah, nothing to worry about. I just managed to get away early today. What you been up to?" Will looked at the boxes and stuff in the bedroom.

"You know me, just having a little sort out. I like to keep things tidy."

"Do you want some help?"

"It's alright, I just need to put these bits back and the rest is for the jumble." Doris indicated the clothes and toys that had not made it into the suitcase but already Will was helping and soon the bed had

127

been cleared and a neat stack placed on the ottoman. Doris closed the attic hatch and went to leave the bedroom but Will caught hold of her hand and pulled her towards him.

"I see we've got the house to ourselves. You got time for a dance?" he asked.

"Well," she said, "there's nothing more I need to do for dinner."

"Let's dance then."

He gently brushed her cheek to move a curl of hair off her face and lent in to kiss her. Much may have changed for both of them over the years but they always had each other as a constant. The radio continued playing and Will and Doris danced at the foot of the bed, as happy to be in each other's arms now as they were when they had first met.

COLD WINDS AND RAINY DAYS

2015

20 STORM CLOUDS

Lucy relished the touch of the slight breeze upon her face as she walked across the common with her brother, Harry. They had decided to go out for a while, seeking some air on a stifling hot Sunday afternoon in August and had just bought ice-creams in an attempt to cool down. Harry adjusted his long stride to more of a stroll so that Lucy could keep up and the two of them found their way to a vacant bench and sat down to finish their melting treats. Trying to lick the fast-moving vanilla drips from her cone, Lucy looked at London's skyline spread out in front of them.

"Still impressive isn't it? No matter how many times you've seen it." Harry motioned towards the view, taking a big slurp of the cookies and cream scoop that he had chosen from the flavour menu chalked on the board at the side of the café counter hatch.

"Oh yes," replied Lucy. "I've tried to draw it several times but I can't quite capture it."

"I'm sure you can. You shouldn't doubt yourself so much."

"Maybe."

"Trust me, Lucy. You've got a talent for it."

Lucy would like to have believed Harry and to feel more confident in her artwork, actually in herself generally. She wondered why it came so easily to Harry. He had always had a belief that he could do whatever he set out to do and generally he had. Growing up, he and James had been a formidable force, twin boys full of energy and exuberance making an impression upon any room they entered. Conversations were regularly hijacked by one or the other of them, or most likely a combination of the two of them, with each one continuing on from the other in that strange way that twins often seem to adopt, almost finishing each other's thoughts and sentences. Once Lucy was old enough to join in conversations, she frequently felt unable to fit into their world, partly due to the age gap and partly the 'twin understanding' that they had between them.

Harry and James still had it but the bond seemed less obvious now. As boys they had wanted to do the same things all the time but as adolescence crept in, they began to develop separate interests and wanted to show that they were individuals too. With different choices at school came different career paths, Harry in sports physiotherapy and James in marketing but they were both still living at home and both still teased Lucy in that annoying older sibling way that typified their relationship. So it was quite something for her to hear Harry praising her.

"Anyway, you'll know soon enough. All that hard work you've done, bound to get great results for your art and the rest of them." Harry lent back on the bench with his legs outstretched on the path in front of him, one foot resting on the other. As if in deep thought for a moment, he scratched his bearded chin and then clasped his hands behind his head, sighing before he continued. "Probably get the best results of the family."

"Okay, who are you and what have you done with my brother?" joked Lucy.

"What do you mean?"

"I'm not used to compliments, Harry. You usually criticise me."

"Nonsense. Advise you, maybe. Tease you, definitely. But what do you expect?"

"Why?"

"You're the youngest, Lucy. And of course, you are a girl!" He laughed and narrowly avoided the dig in the ribs that she attempted to give him in retaliation for this last comment. "See – too slow."

"I'm too hot to argue," conceded Lucy.

On that matter, Harry agreed with her. The two of them moved on from their rest spot and headed for the tree line, passing by the scattering of couples and family groups all making the most of the humid Sunday afternoon, locals and tourists alike enjoying the space and the views of Greenwich and beyond.

The dappled shade of the path through the trees offered a little respite from the heat and their conversation turned to how they had noticed that Dad had made a few more visits to see Gran over the summer. In fact, Lucy was pleased that all of her brothers had made a point of popping in to see Gran since the day spent clearing her house a few months ago. Maybe that tangible event had made Gran's reality more obvious to them. Lucy felt that it had given them a little pang of guilt that they hadn't made as much effort before. Then again, they were all wrapped up in their busy lives.

All three of her brothers had full time jobs and friends to socialise with. Harry played rugby most Sunday mornings during the season and regularly made use of his gym membership in-between his shifts. James was partial to a craft beer with his colleagues after work at the various hipster bars in the area and often slept in at the weekends to recharge his batteries from his hard weeks of work and play. Then there was Tom, Lucy's oldest brother. He had moved out last year and was now slowly setting up his home and life with his girlfriend, Amy. They all had different priorities to Lucy and to be honest, she had always been the one closest to Gran.

In many ways, Gran had been more of a mother figure to Lucy in her early years than her mum, Jane. It took a long while for Jane to bond with Lucy, much more so than with all of her boys. Having to return to full time work just a few months after Lucy's birth meant that childcare arrangements, by necessity, included Lucy spending a lot of time with her grandparents. On such days, Lucy was welcomed with the big smiles and kind hearts that Doris and Will always had ready for visitors, though they seemed to have a little more of both for their granddaughter.

Walking in the relative coolness of the trees, Lucy and Harry were happy to linger there a while. Though they had talked about the visits to Green Meadows they both had avoided bringing up how much Doris was deteriorating. They both knew it, as did their father, but they chose to focus on other subjects. Abruptly their conversation stopped and Lucy and Harry stood still for a moment. There had been a sudden drop in the temperature and a stillness in the air that arrived from nowhere. Even the birds seemed to pause to take notice.

"Storm's brewing," said Harry.

Whilst they had been walking beneath the trees they had not noticed the grey clouds that were rolling in from the city or the gradual emptying of the park as other visitors had thought to start making their way home and away from the incoming rain. Thunder rumbled and Lucy exchanged glances with Harry.

"Shall we make a run for it?" Lucy asked.

"Nah, probably won't last long," said Harry. "Let's just stay here under cover."

Lucy was exhilarated by it all, standing under their tree canopy, mentally counting the seconds between glimpses of lightning and the accompanying thunder, as both encroached ever closer. She had never been afraid of thunder like some children are, far from it. Instead her mum would call her away from the window to be out of harm's way, when all she wanted was to watch the lightning doing battle with the dark clouds.

It did not take long for the stillness of the air to be replaced with a downpour of rain, bringing the trees around them to life - the fresh smell of leaves and grass awakened by the raindrops, the spattering of branches, the hues of green all damp and glistening. Lucy gave Harry a sideways glance and then broke cover. Harry followed suit and they both emerged onto the grass, laughing as the rain refreshed their skin and soaked into their hair and clothes.

"You're mad," laughed Harry.

"Sometimes," she replied, twirling around in the rain. "But doesn't it feel great?"

"Yes, yes it does." Harry allowed himself to join in a few twirls until they both felt a little dizzy. "Crazy Lucy."

"Maybe I am."

"Come on, Crazy. Let's get home and dry off before dinner."

Harry linked his arm through Lucy's in a show of camaraderie usually reserved for James. They giggled and began making their way back across the park, their clothes drenched and raindrops cascading down their faces. It had been a good afternoon.

21 BITS AND PIECES

Sam was doing his best to pick up the broken pieces of the cup that Doris had thrown across the bedroom in frustration. His voice was firm but calm in his endeavor to reassure Doris that there was nothing to worry about.

"You just stay there on your bed for a moment, Doris, until I pick this all up."

"I'm sorry... I can't do it." Doris tried to explain, tapping her clenched fists repeatedly against her thighs.

"No matter, we'll soon get it all cleared up," Sam replied.

Doris was gradually losing her depth perception and that, along with her arthritis, meant that even everyday actions like placing her cup back on to her bed tray required a lot of effort and patience. Although Doris had always been known for both, particularly when nursing Will through the dark days of his cancer, she struggled now to hang onto these qualities. Having tried twice to return her tea safely to the tray, something had snapped for a moment. When these moments occurred, she seemed to shock herself. Indeed anyone who knew her well would not have recognised the behaviour that bubbled to the surface. But of course, it was all out of her control.

She lay her head back on her propped up pillows and sighed deeply. Closing her eyes for a moment, she pressed her hands into the bed sheets on either side of her body, willing her fingers to spread out and feel the comfort of the cotton fabric beneath them. Focused on her hands and the bed, the other bits and pieces of the room stopped tumbling around in her mind and she felt less anxious, less troubled.

"That's all sorted now, Doris," said Sam, seeking to reassure her. "All good as new."

"Thank-you, dear."

Doris watched Sam put his dustpan and brush onto a cleaning trolley that stood just outside her bedroom doorway. He had picked up all the debris and wiped down the wallpaper with a soapy cloth.

"I'll just get rid of this trolley and then I'll be back. Perhaps we'll take a little walk together then?"

He did not wait for an answer and Doris made no effort to move from the bed. She had tried going for a few walks recently and been in trouble for it. She was not sure why but there was always somebody ready to stop her by the front door and bring her back to bed. She wanted to walk by the sea or across a field where there were apples but she could never quite find them.

She remembered there was contraband in her room. Doris pulled open the drawer of her bedside cabinet and found a half packet of wine gums inside, alongside her glasses and a large print book that she could no longer follow the story line in. Doris laughed and sent the remaining sweets tumbling onto her bed covers in her haste to open the packet. Furtively, she scooped them up and began sucking two of them at once. A lot of her food tasted the same lately but she craved sugary snacks with the relish of a toddler gaining unsupervised access to a chocolate cake. It took only a few minutes for her to finish the sweets. Just in time for Sam to return to her bedroom doorway.

"You all set then, Doris?" Sam was smiling as he set her walking frame ready. "Time to get out of your room for a while."

Sam helped Doris along the corridor, into the lift and down to the garden room. They passed Bob and Violet, a couple of Green Meadows' long term residents, who were helping each other to complete a jigsaw puzzle whilst they sipped their 3 o'clock tea. Doris used to enjoy doing jigsaws on Sunday afternoons, especially in the colder months when the weather dictated that more time was spent indoors. But she had neither the patience nor the dexterity to complete one now. She remembered unwrapping a Christmas gift from her son one year, a jigsaw depicting a landscape with a steam train heading towards a tunnel in the hillside. It had taken a long time and a family effort to complete the puzzle, everyone pausing to do a little more every time they passed it on the kitchen table. Where was that family now?

"You off for a walk, Doris?" asked Bob.

"Oh yes, dear. I think so," she muttered and continued to focus on pushing her walking frame forward.

"Going to take a spin around the garden," chipped in Sam. "How's that puzzle going, Violet?"

"Coming together, Sam, coming together." Violet lifted her teacup and nodded at the puzzle picture spreading out before her.

Doris was halfway out of the door by now and ready to head down the ramp into the garden. She took a deep breath at the top of the ramp and let the autumn colours of the garden register in her mind before setting off on her lap. The russets and golds clung to the trees that had yet to shed their leaves across the lawn and a few deep red chrysanthemums stood proud in the first flower bed they passed. Much of the garden was already falling into the hibernation mode that nature instigates for the winter months ahead. Sam helped Doris to steer her way past the gardener, Sharon, who was engrossed in her weekly battle to rake the leaves.

"Afternoon, Sharon," greeted Sam, "never-ending task, that one."

"Oh yes, one of many. Bit of pruning to do yet before I get my bulbs in."

"That'll be nice, won't it, Doris? A few spring daffodils?"

"Daffodils? Mum's favourite," said Doris and carried on walking a little further. A particularly brave robin hopped across the path in front of Doris and flew up to the nearby bird feeder. She stopped to watch. Did she feed the birds somewhere? There was a park and a man by her side but she could not recall his name. She looked down to find she was holding hands with a boy in a duffel coat. They were off to feed the ducks and he smiled up at her and the man. But it was no good, she couldn't find their names and the faces were fading.

"Shall we sit here for a bit?" asked Sam. He thought that Doris might need a rest as she had stopped by the bird feeder but it was only whilst she tried to piece together the pictures in her head.

"No, no. Keep walking. I'll do my lap." Doris persevered with her steps, pushing the frame and keeping her eye on the path ahead. "Round and round the garden, like a teddy bear…"

Sam smiled and joined in with her song, three more times in fact as Doris repeated the nursery rhyme that had found its way into her mind, until they turned the last corner of the path and sat themselves down on one of the wooden benches.

"You love a good sing song, don't you?"

"Yes, dear. Used to sing at the pub and play piano."

A random moment of clarity allowed Doris to see the Eight Bells, beer glasses perched on top of the piano and her fingers on the keys. There was laughter and chatter and friendship. Then, just as quickly as the image had formed, it was gone. And she was alone again. Alone in her thoughts and cold.

Sam saw her shiver and stood up from the bench.

"Let's get you warmed up inside. Soon be tea time."

Doris did not raise an objection and shuffled off with her frame, past Sharon's pile of leaves, towards the warmth of the garden room and a beaker of tea.

FROM A DISTANCE

(1986)

22 PEACHES AND CREAM

Two wine glasses stood alongside a bowl of crisps on the table.
Nothing extraordinary about that on a Saturday evening but the box
of items perched nearby on the kitchen worktop hinted at something
a little different. Doris had been looking forward to this evening all
week. Maggie had jumped at the chance to be enlisted into making
bridal favours with her and both of them were eager to shoo the men
out of the way and begin the gossip and giggles and anticipation of
Andrew's wedding next week.

A positive energy emerged whenever Maggie walked into a room,
rubbing off on anyone who happened to be there and Doris was
keen to bask in that tonight. Between them, they made no apologies
for hurrying Will and Fred out of the house and on their way to join
in Andrew's Stag Do at the local pub. An hour or so earlier, Doris
had been less keen to hurry Andrew on his way to meet up with his
mates. She felt a pang of sadness watching him set off, the boy she
had doted on all these years, now a man soon to embark upon
married life – how was she old enough for this to be happening?

Anyway, it was now time to focus on the serious matter in hand –
having a good chinwag.

"Shall I pour the wine, then?" asked Maggie. "I've been looking
forward to tonight."

"Oh yes, me too. A whole evening of girl talk – without the men
around. Pour away."

"Amen to that."

They laughed and raised their glasses in a shared act of companionship. Chatting away, Doris started to lay out the contents of the cardboard box from the kitchen worktop.

"T'is there anything else you need help with for the wedding?" asked Maggie. Age had not knocked her flair for enthusiasm nor her ability to jump on board and offer support should it be needed any time.

"Not really. I'm grateful to have this to do, truth be told. Jane's family insisted on sorting most of the wedding, parents of the bride – their prerogative, I guess."

"Ah well, I'm sure these will look super by the time we've finished with them. Now tell me the plan."

Doris began unfurling a roll of peach coloured tulle as Maggie picked up a couple of cardboard templates and the dressmaking scissors. Maggie held up an edge of the tulle for inspection "I like the colour. It's very pretty."

"Yes, all chosen to coordinate. Peach netting and cream ribbon – just what Jane asked for, of course."

"Of course."

"I'm thinking, we cut out the circles of net first, then add the sugared almonds."

"And tie them all up with the ribbon." Maggie jumped in before Doris could finish.

"Exactly."

"Best to do the cutting before we've had too many glasses of this," she laughed, pushing her wine glass out of reach and away from the spool of ribbon.

The two friends settled down to their task, cutting circles. Doris explained how she had stood for ages in Charlie's fabric shop, comparing shades of tulle and widths of ribbon wanting to make sure that she had the best she could afford. Charlie's was a cavern of a shop, narrowing as customers progressed to the back of it. It was easy to become overwhelmed by the rolls of materials stacked upon each other, satins and cottons, patterns a plenty, buttons and bows, lace and spools of ribbon on rods, arranged by width and shade of colour. She had been grateful when Charlie had stepped in to suggest how much of each she would need for the sixty favours.

"And what about you, what colour are you wearing? Green has always suited you, Dot, but I'm not sure for a wedding – is that bad luck?"

"I don't know about that but don't worry, it's not green. I've got quite a simple dress, a floral print – don't want to upstage the mother of the bride."

"And why not? You're the mother of the groom, just as important in my book and bound to look better anyway."

"Well I'm not in competition. Just glad to be sharing the day."

"Indeed. Talking of sharing the day, Fred tells me that Lillian's coming over for the wedding. Isn't that just grand?"

"Oh yes, I can't wait to see her."

Maggie took the wine bottle out of the fridge and started refilling their glasses. "When's she getting here?"

"Flight's due at Heathrow early on Thursday morning. We're going to pick her up and take her out for lunch."

"Splendid."

"She's here for a couple of weeks. We'll have you and Fred over for dinner one evening, after the wedding. More of a chance to catch up properly."

"We'd love that. Be just like old times, when we used to chat into the early hours. Do you remember?"

"You're going back a bit now."

"True, I need my bed too much these days. Still it'll be a treat to see her again, hear what life's like across the pond."

"No doubt she'll have many tales to tell us."

"Oh yes. Now, Dot, how many of these are we stuffing in these circles? Have you been given strict instructions on the quota of almonds?"

Doris started laughing at how direct Maggie was. Had it been so obvious how little part she felt she and Will were taking in this wedding? It was certainly true that Jane was a confident woman, not afraid to voice her opinions on how things should be done. But then again, it was her wedding day and a bride likes to create their own fairytale. It was just that Doris had never been one for making a big fuss and there was quite a lot going into this day that seemed over the top to her.

"You know that every mother would feel the same?"

"What do you mean, Maggie?"

"Letting go. No bride is going to look after a son the way that you would."

"Oh, Andrew doesn't need looking after anymore."

"True. But that doesn't stop you wanting the best for him or feeling that you're a bit redundant."

"You are too direct for your own good sometimes, Maggie."

"Maybe. Are we counting sugared almonds or shall I just stuff 'em in?"

"Let's see how we go. Make it up as we go along. Thanks, Maggie."

"For what?"

"Just thanks."

Doris thought about how their friendship had developed over the years. Maggie had a lot of wisdom beneath that bubbly exterior and she was usually right about most things. In her direct way, she had touched a nerve. For whatever reason, Doris was having a hard time letting go of Andrew, even though she knew he was happy. She hoped that happiness would last for him and Jane, just like it had done for her and Will.

"You're welcome, Dot. Now pass the crisps, I need to soak up a bit of this wine."

The evening continued in a similar way - wine, crisps, chatting and stuffing almonds into pretty little bundles, ready for the big day next week. Mainly there was lots of reminiscing. Doris recalled the dinner disaster on the night that Andrew had first brought Jane round to meet them, when Jane had not liked the recipe she had tried for the first time in an effort to impress and how she had then dropped the trifle. There had been cream all over the kitchen and she had felt so embarrassed. Maggie, in her inimitable way, brushed it all off in a way that made them both laugh heartily.

Indeed, it did seem funny to recall, though she could not see it that way at the time. One thing was certain, she had not made the best first impression. Still, that was a couple of years ago now. Soon Andrew and Jane would be cooking for themselves, along with everything else that goes into making their new home life. Though, she had to concede, they might not be making trifle.

23 THE LUNCH STOP

When it came to birthdays or Christmas, Will usually kept things simple. He might pick up some flowers or a box of Black Magic chocolates for Doris, but mostly he preferred to put some money in a card so that she could choose a few treats for herself. He always said it was better that way because he was likely to choose the wrong things. With that pattern established, it was quite a surprise when Doris discovered his plans to mark her fiftieth birthday. Will had booked them into a countryside guest house for a long weekend and they had set off shortly after breakfast on the Friday morning.

Doris had packed the night before, careful to include a range of layers with her usual forethought to plan for all possibilities and cover the many options that the English weather can conjure up in May. But their drive this morning saw them emerge from a warm city into expanding space on either side of the road, under a sunlit canopy of blue. Enough blue sky to make a whole fleet a new outfit let alone just a single pair of sailor's trousers, as her mother's saying would have been. It was odd how certain sayings stayed with Doris, even from long ago, at a random moment one might pop into her head along with a fading image of the person who used to say it – usually her mother or Aunty Joan.

"Almost lunchtime, be nice to stop for a while, don't you think?" explained Will when he pulled off the Sussex A-road to park the car.

"Good idea," said Doris, happy to let Will take the lead. Alongside the small car park, there were a few picnic benches placed for the convenience of pausing motorists but beyond these, a pathway led past trees towards a viewing point. Ever the outdoor enthusiast, Will had suggested a walk to stretch their legs before eating their lunch and so they set off away from the picnic area.

As they had adjusted to being just a couple again over the past three years since Andrew's wedding, they had enjoyed time spent walking together at weekends. Usually though, that was closer to home. A walk around one of the local parks mostly, or on some Sundays they would catch a bus up to Charing Cross and walk along the Embankment for the afternoon.

Here though, away from the city, the air felt different. They both loved the chance to be where there was more space, more green and more time to notice nature's details. Will pointed out certain tress or plants of interest along their route. In places, gnarled twists of tree roots broke through the earth to stretch across their path. Sometimes a patch of nettles and brambles threatening to snag passing clothing required evasive action in order to be passed safely but Doris and Will embraced it all.

"Are you okay, Dot? Mind your step."

"Don't worry about me – not too old for a little ramble, not yet anyway."

"Here, take my hand."

Together they made their way up the grassy incline that led from the more wooded area to the viewpoint at the top. The view that rewarded them was well worth the walk. A white stone marked the summit, with a bronze engraved plate set into the top of it, indicating names and distances of various points around their vista as the South Downs spread out before them. They spent some time registering the beauty of it all and then walked a few steps back down from the stone, to nestle themselves into the hillside.

Sat side by side, Will took out a flask of tea and a Tupperware box which Doris had packed earlier with their lunch. Will poured each of them a cup of tea. Sipping tea and content in the moment, minutes past before either of them spoke.

"Beautiful day for it, eh Dot?"

"Yes. Can see for miles."

Doris looked past the 'sailor's trousers' to the few patches of white clouds hanging high above them.

"I still like to watch the clouds. Reminds me of when we were kids," said Doris. "Lil and I used to see what shapes we could find."

Will looked up, to join in the quest. "Reckon that's an island there, can you see it?"

"Yes, a treasure island. At least, that's the sort of story that Lillian would make up for it."

"A treasure island it is then. One with pirates and vagabonds."

"Of course." Her sunny smile rejoiced in the playfulness of their conversation and how relaxed Will was, away from work and routine.

"We'll have to play this game with Tom when he's a bit older."

"When we're allowed to see him."

"Now, Dot. It's not that bad," admonished Will. "I guess they like it just being the three of them sometimes."

"Maybe."

"Remember when we were just getting used to our little family of three?"

"Hard to think - that was so long ago."

"True."

"I'm sorry Will, it would just be nice to be round that a bit more."

"I know, love."

"Sometimes it feels like we might as well be on the other side of the world, instead of just across the river."

"Let's not worry about it today, love."

"No, you're right. I don't want anything to spoil this weekend. Can't believe you've gone to so much trouble and all without me knowing."

"Glad I can still surprise you." With that comment, Will put his arm around her shoulders and lent in to kiss her cheek. "Now, let's eat. I'm famished."

He snapped open the lid of their lunch box and unwrapped the Clingfilm from the rounds of cheese and pickle sandwiches, setting them down between the two of them. Will planned to eat his sandwiches first, saving his slice of gala pie to savour last. His smile between bites reflected his satisfaction at being able to make a fuss of Doris, just for a few days, giving her the attention she deserved.

"Another cup of tea, love?"

"Yes please."

She passed him her cup and continued nibbling at a square of sandwich as she looked out to the distant tree line. All who had been close to her over the years, now had a distance from her of one sort or another. All except, Will. How special it was to still be alongside each other.

They did not hurry their lunch, after all there was no need to rush today. They could not check in to their guest house until later. They chatted a little more but mostly enjoyed the stillness of the afternoon and the comfort of each other. Sat together in the sunshine, then holding hands as Will helped Doris steady herself again, to pick their steps back down the hill to the woodland path and the car beyond.

The weekend would be filled with little moments like that. Those were what mattered most to Doris. More than the dinners at the guest house, the cakes in a village tea shop or the beautiful earrings he had surprised her with when she opened her birthday card on the Sunday morning. Those were all special moments too and Doris had not expected any of them from Will.

What she had come to expect though, was for Will to always have a hand ready to steady her along their path together. At least that would remain so for a few more years, with lunch stops and garden walks and more grandchildren yet to come.

24 SNAPSHOTS

Years tumbled past in the way they do, almost twenty years, marked by holidays, celebrations and the little highlights that life allows us across time. With all of it, Doris and Will embraced the good times with their customary smiles and laughter and stood formidably together to face the challenge of any low points that came their way. Their retirement coincided with the new millennium, by which time they had been blessed with four grandchildren and several nieces and nephews on Will's side of the family and they reveled in the time they got to spend with any of them.

They did not have snapshots of all the family moments, nobody really does. But Doris had a lot of them stored away in her memory. There was the time that Will had helped Tom to ride his bike without stabilisers, running behind him along the pathway in the local park. Days at the seaside with Andrew, Jane and the boys, splashing on the water's edge, trying to skim stones on the waves and rounded off by sitting on the beach eating chips with a vinegar tinged sea breeze in their faces. There were the smiles she shared with Will when the phone call from the hospital announced the arrival of their precious granddaughter, Lucy.

Countless Christmas dinners, handmade birthday cards, celebrations and meals out, happy faces round their kitchen table tucking into her treacle sponge and custard, bedtime stories and much, much more. The list was long. Nobody ever has photographs of all of it, all the stuff that really matters. And nobody really stops to think about all of that stuff – until it disappears.

***

Will was gone. He slipped away quietly in his sleep, in his own bed, two weeks after Doris and Lucy returned from their Boscombe holiday. The Macmillan nurse had sat with him a while that evening and shared a pot of tea with Doris, reassuring her that Will's pain relief was working and he was comfortable. The strength that Doris had found these past two years had been quite remarkable, but Doris did not see it that way. It was just her duty, the natural thing to do. To anyone who asked, she always had the same response.

"In sickness and in health, you know. It's my turn to look out for Will now."

Doris was pleased that he had managed to see out his last days within his own home, their little place on Brewer Street that they both loved. Now, she saw him in the shadows. A trick of the light and her mind would see him at the foot of the stairs. A sunny moment in the back yard and he was watering the plants. Some mornings she had put two mugs by the kettle when making breakfast. This afternoon, she sat looking at his empty chair.

She was glad to be having company in a while, for a little support. Support that had come from an unlikely source. Jane was driving over with Lucy for the afternoon. Doris had never had a particularly close relationship with Jane, but she had to admit that lately, she had seen her daughter-in-law in a new light. She had always thought that Jane felt she was better than them, that she had married into rougher stock. It had taken a long time for the bonds of family to pull them closer together but, with Will gone, Doris saw a softer side. Jane's practical, no-nonsense approach had provided a strength that both she and Andrew used as a rock to anchor themselves upon and Doris was grateful.

The spare key turned in the lock and her two visitors arrived to break the silence in the room. Lucy spoke first and ran over to give Doris a hug.

"Hi Gran."

"Hello, my lovely. Now come and sit down for a while."

"Shall I go and put the kettle on, make us all a cup of tea?" asked Jane. "I've brought biscuits – your favourites, I think. Garibaldis."

Jane rummaged in her bag until she found the biscuits and held them up for approval.

"Thanks, Jane. I'm not sure if there are any others in my tin, but I do like a Garibaldi."

Lucy was used to Gran getting out the biscuit tin whenever she went round. It had a red lid with a tarnished metal knob on top that wobbled slightly as you pulled it to reveal the contents inside. There were always two or three different types of biscuits to choose from and sometimes, if she was lucky, there would be a foil wrapped tea cake. On those days, Lucy would check if she could have it and then sit smoothing out the red and silver foil wrap, long after she had devoured the chocolate covered marshmallow treat.

"Have you run out of biscuits then, Gran?"

"Oh, well maybe, Lucy. I've lost track of the groceries a bit, that's all."

"Not to worry," said Jane. "I'll see what I can find." She disappeared into the kitchen and filled the kettle, then started looking in the cupboards to check what food was there. "I'll make a list, see what you need. I can pop up the road after a cuppa and get a few bits of shopping for you."

"Don't go to any trouble, not on my account."

"Nonsense! No trouble at all."

Doris knew not to argue with her daughter-in-law and anyway, she was pleased to accept her offer. They sipped their tea and enjoyed a couple of biscuits, then Jane left with her shopping list and carrier bags from the stock that Doris kept under the stairs.

"I've got something for us to look at," began Doris.

Lucy looked up from her cup, wondering what it could be. Doris placed a box full of old photographs on the coffee table and started to spread out a few of its contents.

"Thought you might like to see these. I don't really know how far back they go."

"Ooh, let's see what we can find, Gran."

"Some of them have dates and stuff written on the back of them. Goodness me, Lucy, I didn't realise there were so many."

Lucy sat herself on the floor with her legs tucked under the coffee table. She started making rows of photographs, separating the colour ones from the black and white images. Every so often she would find one of particular interest, turn it over to search for details penciled on the reverse and ask Gran questions about it, as if piecing together a grand mystery of the past. She liked the names of the different friends and relatives – Great Grandmothers Daisy and Martha, an Uncle Bert and an Aunty Joan, a Ted, a Polly, a Maggie and an Irish Mary.

There were some very faded ones from year's back that reminded Lucy of the pictures she had seen in some of her school history lessons. Although the colour of more recent shots brought more life into the images, Lucy was drawn to the oldest photos in the box. She and Doris kept going, surveying the photographs a few at a time.

"This one's your Dad, Lucy. Look at his curls." Doris smiled at Lucy's reaction.

"Look Gran, that's me with you and Grandad, by the river. Do you remember? You took me on a boat trip." Lucy looked over to see Gran reaching for a tissue from the box beside her armchair. "I'm sorry, Gran. Shall we put them away?"

"Don't be sorry love. We're lucky to have the pictures, to have all these people and places in one box."

"Yes, Gran. I think it's very special."

"Then I think you should look after it."

"What?"

"The box, Lucy. Will you keep it safe for me?"

"Don't you want to have all the people here, so you can keep looking at them?"

"Maybe, in a while. I tell you what, you keep them, like a treasure box. If I want them, I know where they are and I know you'll be careful with them."

"Always, Gran."

"I know, Lucy. You're a good girl. Shall we have another cup of tea, and more biscuits?"

Doris went out to the kitchen to make more tea whilst Lucy collected up the photographs and carefully replaced the lid on the box.

"I'll come and help you, Gran."

FADING PICTURES

(2016)

25 JANUARY BLUES

They had eaten in shifts this evening. Lucy and Harry welcomed the chili con carne that Jane had cooked when she had got in from work and were keen to demolish their portions. Andrew was stuck at Victoria station, due to a signal failure causing delays and James would be working late as usual, so Jane decanted their portions into some take-away tubs that she kept handy for such occasions. They could both pop their meal into the microwave once they got in without anyone having to cook from scratch again. Jane liked the efficiency of that. At this first sitting, the three of them sat together to share a little of their day.

"Can you grab the sour cream, Harry?" asked Jane, adding some rice to each of their plates.

"Yeh. Looks great, Mum. Should warm us up."

"I hope so. Wintry out there." Jane passed a plate across to Harry. "I'm glad to be inside."

Lucy took her plateful and began to tuck in. "Hope Dad won't be too long."

"He's used to it, happens a lot," said Jane. "How was college today?"

"Good thanks. I've got a few bits of work to get through this week, might do some after dinner."

"Great," Harry jibed. "I get to hog the telly then."

"Only if you load the dishwasher first," said Jane. "It's your turn tonight."

Lucy and Harry were expected to take their turn in a few chores around the house. James was also supposed to do his fair share but he was often working late on his days, the subject of some debate and sibling tension at times. Mostly though, arguments were avoided and each of the five adults living in the house found their own space and routines. Lucy's involved a lot of retreating to the little creative oasis of her bedroom.

With dinner finished and Harry busy loading the dishwasher, Jane gathered up a few notes to look through for work and Lucy went upstairs for the evening. She should have been finishing a college project but instead, she took out the scrapbook journal from her desk drawer. Much had happened since Lucy began documenting her family in this last year. The pages were slowly filling up, when time allowed her to focus on it. Within its pages, her illustrations wove their way around the thoughts that she had committed to paper. It had been a therapeutic exercise to dip into initially, but the further Gran had deteriorated, the more impetus the project had taken on, frequently beckoning Lucy back to complete it.

She had selected a few photographs from the box that sat on her bookshelf, Gran's box that Lucy now felt duty bound to protect – as though she were a custodian of memories. In reality the scrapbooking project had become a memory document, linking fragments together in a tangible attempt to hang onto them. Just like clinging to the strings of a bunch of balloons on a windy day, every so often one would get away and float off towards the clouds. Lucy did not want them all to escape.

Sometimes she used a remembered quote from a story shared by one of the family, sometimes a picture created from her own feelings. She had chosen not to paste any of Lillian's letters in there but odd phrases from them came to mind as she drew and some found their way onto the pages. After all she had read through the old letters and postcards several times now, a collection that spanned about twenty years and became more sporadic as the years went on. In reading them, Lucy had imagined the life that Lillian was creating for herself. As a reader does with all good books, she was left wanting to know more, beyond the last letter in the tin, to fill in the details about Great Aunt Lillian.

"There's a freedom here that I have not felt before."

This line from a letter from Canada in the mid-seventies had inspired Lucy to devote a double-page, carefully writing it across both in italic font before letting her imagination loose along with her watercolours. It had struck a chord with her and as she created the pages around it, she thought how being absorbed in her artwork was her own freedom, her escape from the troubling parts of her life. Headphones in, drawing or with paint flowing across the paper in front of her, Lucy entered the space in her mind where the details of everyday life dissolved away. She could twirl her kaleidoscope view of the world until it settled into the pattern she preferred. The best of Gran's stories, the nostalgia of a photograph, the edited show reel of a family's life.

Lucy had the scrapbook open at the page where her soft pencil sketch of Gran looked back at her. Caught on a cheery day with a wry smile casting its infectious spell, this likeness was a favourite of Lucy's garden room sketches and she had captioned it with a phrase from the story Gran was telling at the time.

"And we could see for miles…"

Such carefree snapshots were harder to find these past few months. Christmas had been a poignant contradiction for Lucy, all the while feeling that she was juggling emotions. Balancing the celebration of discovering that she would become an aunty in the new year and the warmth of time spent as a family, with knowing that just an hour spent at Green Meadows on Christmas morning was all that Gran could manage without becoming overwhelmed. Driving back home with her father for their festive dinner had been an eerie experience, passing along unusually quiet roads, both of them unable to shake the unspoken thought in their minds that this was probably Gran's last Christmas.

Once back from their visit, Lucy and her father did their best to throw themselves into the day's festivities. Tom and Amy had already arrived and were placing gifts under the tree whilst everyone was chatting and generally bustling around. Thinking back now to this scene, Lucy realised that Tom had been bubblier than usual, obviously excited to share his news. He was almost overly helpful in the kitchen with the dinner preparations, getting everything in place on the table before making sure everybody had some fizz in their glass, ready to toast his announcement. All except Amy, that is, who sipped orange juice as everyone raised glasses to a Happy Christmas and the expected baby.

Much of the discussion in-between courses and the pulling of crackers centered on how Tom and Amy would manage the months ahead. They were almost finished with decorating their flat, then they planned to work out how to accommodate a cot and all the paraphernalia that comes with a baby. Listening to her eldest brother's plans and knowing he was going to be a father, somehow made Lucy feel more grown-up. She had to admit she had done a lot of growing up this past year.

Lucy's exam results last August had been enough to see her start a foundation year at Art College which had meant meeting new people and trying new things and generally pushing herself out of her comfort zone but she was enjoying the challenge. She still fitted in her weekly trips to Gran, keeping the familiarity of this routine as one comfort amongst her struggle to accept the realities of Gran's illness. It was reassuring in some ways, that other family members were taking time to visit more, finding their own slots each month to pop in, even if Gran did not seem to know who they were or indeed remember that they had been.

The sketch before her did not tell the whole story, not by a long shot. But Lucy loved the moment it captured – Gran's smile as she remembered a day out and the connection between them as she shared the memory with Lucy. The wind was gaining force tonight and rattled the branches of the tree against the bedroom window. Neither Andrew nor James were home yet. Lucy yawned and absentmindedly flicked through the last pages of the scrapbook before closing it. There were only a couple of pages left to fill. She might save one of them to include the newest addition to the family, in a few months' time. As for the last page, she was not sure, she would give it a little more thought, but not tonight.

A text message pinged on her phone.

Oi, Lu. Want a cuppa t?

It was Harry, texting her from downstairs rather than coming up to ask her in person. Lucy smiled and decided that she needed a bit more comfort than tea gave.

I'll come down, don't worry.

Pulling the tie of her fluffy dressing gown around her tighter, she left her bedroom to head off to the kitchen and make a hot chocolate and raid the biscuit tin. Winter nights always felt better with a mug of hot chocolate.

26 PUZZLES

"Shall we park you up here then, Doris, ready for your visitor?" Sam did not wait for agreement from Doris but continued in his cheery way to jolly her along, settling her into her favourite spot in the garden room and put the wheelchair brake on. He believed that Doris responded to her view of the garden each afternoon as a visual, if not physical exercise, now that her legs refused to cooperate with her most of the time. On warmer afternoons, he would wheel her around the garden path a few times so that she could feel the air against her face and listen for melody in the birdsong.

From her spot today, Doris turned her attention between a sparrow pecking for worms on the lawn beyond the window and what was going on around her in the room. A new resident whose name she could not remember stood for a while trying to make sense of his new surroundings before Sam encouraged him to move on to the television room. Bob and Violet had just embarked upon a new jigsaw puzzle. They sat at their usual table with the lid of the puzzle propped up against the wall, chatting casually as they sifted through the different puzzle pieces to find all the straight edges ready to outline the village scene.

Dotted around the rest of the room were a further three chairs, more cosy than those at the puzzle table. Armchairs that looked lived in, each with tales that they could tell of the many people who had sat in them over the years. Faded but functional in offering a place to rest for a while. Doris slowly became aware that Lucy had pulled one of them closer to sit down beside her wheelchair.

"Hi, Gran. Sam told me you were in here. How are you doing today?"

Doris looked over at Lucy and a half smile of recognition flickered at the corners of her mouth. She felt tired a lot of the time now and words became harder to articulate but she nodded in Lucy's direction.

"I've brought something to show you today."

Lucy took her scrapbook out from her bag, excited to show Gran the pages, to read a little of it to her, hoping that some of the content might spark a few memories. She knew it might be a futile exercise, so much had slipped away lately, but as Gran had inspired much of her project, Lucy was determined to share it with her.

"What you got there, Lucy" asked Sam, who had returned with a beaker of tea for Doris. "Is it your work?"

Over time Sam and the other staff at Green Meadows had got used to seeing Lucy drawing during her visits, sometimes commenting upon how good her sketches were.

"Something I've been working on for a long time, Sam. It's not quite finished but it's got a lot of Gran in it."

"I bet, she is our superstar – quite the character, eh?"

"Maybe she'll recognise bits and pieces."

"Well, she might not tell you so, but I'm sure she'll know some of it, don't you worry about that."

"Thanks, Sam."

With that, Lucy opened the book and Sam went over to speak to Bob and Violet, joining in their puzzle making for a while. Lucy thought about how kind the staff at Green Meadows were. She wondered if she could be as calm and patient as they appeared to be if she had to work there every day. She was unsure that she would manage that.

"Gran, I've made a book about you – well, it's the story of us, all of the family."

Lucy paused. She took a slow breath to quell the tide of water rising in her eyes and then continued.

"Look, Gran. This is a lovely photo of you and Grandad. I'm not sure where it was taken but you're both smiling."

"Smiling," echoed Doris.

Doris stretched her hand towards Lucy and rested it gently on Lucy's arm. She tried hard to listen to the narrative that Lucy gave to each of the pages but it felt akin to tuning into an old radio box. Every so often, a twist of the dial would give some clarity amongst the crackling background and then it was lost again. Nevertheless, she understood the warmth of the gesture and the sense of closeness with this visitor. She sipped from her beaker and watched the swaying branches of the nearest tree in the garden.

Lucy sensed her Gran's tiredness. She had shared quite a few pages and talked far more than she usually did on her visits.

"I can bring the book another day, let's just sit for a while."

She closed the book and started to slot it back into her bag when Louise appeared in the doorway from the corridor and caught Lucy's eye.

"Do you have a moment, Lucy?" asked Louise in that way that those in authority have of turning a question into a command that expects a positive response.

Lucy put her bag to one side and left Gran, to follow Louise a few steps away from the garden room.

"How's Doris doing today, Lucy?"

"She seems okay, perhaps a little tired."

"Do you think she'd manage another visitor?"

Lucy looked perplexed and waited for Louise to continue.

"It's just that we have somebody in reception who's quite keen to see Doris today, says that she's her sister. By all accounts has come a long way, from..."

"Canada," interrupted Lucy, finishing the sentence. The two of them looked at each other momentarily without further comment before Lucy found herself half skipping along beside Louise on their way down the corridor towards the reception desk. Louise hung back at this point, allowing Lucy to approach the visitor and speak first.

"Great Aunt Lillian?"

Lillian turned quickly and held out both hands towards Lucy, a broad smile on her face.

"Yes. Well then, I guess you must be Lucy – my, what a fine young lady you are!

Lucy returned the warmth of this greeting, surprising herself in her willingness to take hold of Lillian's hands, embracing the aunt she had never met.

"Now, Lucy, please drop the Great Aunt bit. Call me Lillian, Lily, Lil, up to you, just take your pick, but Great Aunt, well that just makes me feel so old!"

Lucy laughed. "How about Lily, then?"

"Perfect. So how's my Dottie getting along?"

Lucy shifted her weight from one foot to the other and glanced down.

"It's okay Lucy, not so good eh?"

"Best you come and see, Aunt, I mean, Lily."

"Yes, of course."

Lucy led Lillian along the corridor towards the garden room, somewhat in awe of this woman whom she had spent so much time wondering about, imagined scenarios about and heard her Gran often talking about. Now aged seventy-three but with the energy and poise of somebody much younger, Lillian paused and swooshed her red pashmina across her left shoulder with a flourish. Lucy hesitated to move further and instead found the courage to ask her next question.

"What made you come here, Lily?"

"I had the strangest feeling that I just needed to be here, Lucy. So that's it really, I threw a things in a suitcase, jumped on the next flight and well, here I am."

"Yes, here you are," she led her into the garden room, "and here is Dottie."

27 STEP BY STEP

Lucy had chatted a lot with Lillian since her arrival two weeks ago. There were so many questions that they had of each other, with Lillian quick to work out that of all the family, Lucy had spent the most time with Doris. Although Lillian had mostly lost touch with the family over the last ten years or so, she did know that Doris had been moved to Green Meadows. Andrew had let her know at the time, but Lillian was under the impression this had just been because Doris could no longer manage the house in Brewer Street on her own.

When talking about each other's lives, Lucy had shared her scrapbook with Lillian and found that her aunt was most impressed with the work. In fact, the two of them seemed to strike up an instant bond and Lillian had been quick to invite Lucy to spend the summer over in Canada, pointing out just how much there would be for her to draw and paint there. Lucy's immediate reaction was concern at leaving her Gran for a couple of months but she was also thrilled by the prospect of travelling. It was certainly something to be considered carefully.

Lillian had booked into a hotel not far from Green Meadows and spent a couple of hours with Doris every afternoon. She knew she should have come back to her sister sooner, whilst there would still have been a chance that she might know her. Each afternoon, she sat with Doris. She spent time combing her older sister's hair and talked of times in their youth when they had helped each other that way.

"Shall I help you put your face on?" Lillian asked, reaching for the powder compact on the dressing table. "A little dot of this, here and there. Remember when we used to add our lippy and sneak out before Mum took any notice?"

Doris gave no sign of recognising such anecdotes but she felt comforted by the words. Lilian had not lost her storytelling skills and she held Doris' hand and continued spinning her captivating tales of their childhood and her travels and life overseas. On the days when Lucy joined them, she listened to Lillian's stories too, absorbed in her Aunt's recounts. On one of these afternoons, Lucy found the content idea for the last page of her scrapbook – it would be a sketch of her Gran and her Aunt Lily together, sat on a riverbank on a summer's afternoon.

***

Andrew and Lucy had travelled to Green Meadows together, when the call had come through from Louise, suggesting that it might not be a good idea to wait too long before visiting. The journey had been a blur, with obstinate traffic hindering their progress and what seemed like every red light calling a halt to mock them at each rainy junction. On arrival, Andrew had hastily swung the car onto the gravel driveway and then pulled the hood of his navy cagoule tight, as they made a run for the front door.

Lillian met them there and now that they were all in Doris' bedroom, Lucy looked around at the three generations together. Her brothers were planning to make their way over to see Gran after work but for now it was just the four of them. It took some effort by Lucy and her father to help Doris from her bed to sit in her rocking chair by the bay window but they understood she wanted to get a better look at the garden.

Lucy popped herself at the foot of the bed and placed her soggy drawing bag beside her. Though she had no intention of drawing today, she had just picked it up out of habit as they had rushed out of the door. Lillian preferred to stand for the moment, running the chunky beads of her green necklace through her thumb and forefinger in contemplation. She stood beside the rocking chair and was quiet today. Andrew looked a little out of place on the pink pouffe stool beside the dressing table, trying to make himself comfortable as he picked up the photo frame and looked at the holiday scene – his younger self smiling back at him, stood alongside his mother and father.

"This was a good holiday, Mum, do you remember?" Andrew attempted to engage Doris in conversation. She was unable to follow what he was saying though and instead was saying something about toffees. It was Lucy who understood first and retrieved the toffee tin from Gran's wardrobe. Lucy had put it in a drawer there a few months back when she had brought it to Green Meadows and there it had stayed unmentioned, since Lucy had initially shared its contents with Gran. Today, Gran seemed concerned to know that it was all still there. Lucy placed it on the little coffee table in the bay window and opened the tin. She began narrating her way through each item as she picked them up in turn, with Andrew and Lillian silently listening. Postcards, booties, the ticket. Gran held the faded ticket for a moment as Lucy spoke.

In her rocking chair, crocheted blanket upon her knee and Lucy's wondrous 'treasure box find' placed beside a tray of tea, Doris was now content. The broken connections of life's confusion that usually frustrated Doris were strangely calm this afternoon. Lucy saw this peace reflected in the window pane's rivulets of rain.

With a determined effort Doris pressed the ticket into Lucy's palm, clasped her hand tight and returned her focus to the rain.

"Goodnight, sweetheart…"

It took a lot of strength to form these two words. Doris had steadily grown weaker as the cold months of this New Year passed into the hope of a few spring days. More and more, the dementia was tightening its hold on the free spirit that struggled each day to make connections with Doris. The frustrations of her daily life had slowly worn Doris down, both mentally and physically and she was now a shadow of the woman that previously played out the tunes of her life through her piano music.

Much of that life could have been played in a minor key yet Doris had always been an optimist, a positive energy that touched those around her and brought rewards of kindness in return. At the times in her life when loss made its deepest marks, she had always been able to find a strength to continue from somewhere, whether from deep within or from those around her, always ready to offer support.

Over the past few years, her memories had lost their focus and names had fallen out of her head. Now it took all her strength to lift her beaker to sip her tea and the tunes that played in her mind brought less and less comfort. The toffee tin had sparked an ember of recognition, vague shapes and feelings flickered around her mind trying to consolidate into one clear moment. And as the rain fell outside the window and Lucy spoke about the bus ticket in her hand, the pieces began to link together. There was a couple in the distance, in the shadows and she could hear the rain falling and their laughter floating around her.

Slowly, she curled her fingers around the edge of the blanket on her lap and pulled it closer to her chest, holding it tightly there to keep herself warm. It was a coat, a handsome man's coat protecting her after the dance. Looking through the window pane she started to make out the figure of a broad-shouldered man, standing by the rhododendrons in the garden. He walked towards her holding out an outstretched hand. Doris knew it was time to dance again and all else around her was quiet and still.

EPILOGUE

"Ladies and Gentlemen, my name is Jonathon and I am your chief flight attendant this morning. On behalf of Captain Peters and the entire crew, welcome aboard British Airways flight 243 to Montreal…"

Lucy listened to the rest of the pre-flight announcements as she stowed her bag, fastened her safety belt and let herself sink back into her aisle seat, ready to soak in the experience of her first ever flight. The knot in her stomach tightened when she let that thought register, entwining her excitement with a rising anxiety about take-off. How had she found the courage to embark upon this journey?

A lot had happened in the few months since Gran's funeral, much of it with a momentum of its own, scooping Lucy up along with it. Her beautiful niece, Isla, had arrived to bring joy to the family and a much needed diversion from their collective loss. Lucy also realised that she felt closer to her father than she ever had before and they had spent a nostalgic afternoon on a Kentish steam railway, reminiscing together about each of their favourite memories of her Gran and Granddad.

Alongside all that had taken place, Lucy had completed her foundation year at Art College and accomplished great results, with Harry quick to both congratulate her and gloat in reminding her that he had predicted such things for her. She had been gracious in accepting that and laughed with him over the comments.

Now she had a blank sketch book, ready to fill with her own story. It was time to see what that story might look like. It was fair to say that she was more than a little apprehensive about how this gap year might go but she had decided it would be foolish not to have taken the opportunity. What places would she go to? Who might she meet? Who would believe that the quiet girl who draws would be off on such an adventure?

Lucy adjusted the brooch she had pinned to her jumper and smiled, Gran was with her. She looked across to the nearest window but could only glimpse a little of the scene outside. The plane finished its taxiing as Jonathon completed his announcements and joined the other crew members in clicking their safety belts into place. Lucy's fingernails pressed into the armrests of her chair and she took a couple of deep breaths, ready to hurtle down the runway, leave London behind and soar across the Atlantic…

ABOUT THE AUTHOR

Karen Honnor has always had a love of writing and a dream to sit by the sea, creating stories to share. Like most dreams, there is a danger that they remain as such without ever becoming tangible. Yet in recent years, when circumstances led to her moving away from her long teaching career, Karen determined to use the newly found time and space to pin down a little of her dream and really let the words start flowing.

Over the years, Karen had a few poems published and has written many scripts which were performed by her local community drama group. She began a blog in 2018 and continues to post there, writing about midlife and motherhood and the world as she sees it.

Since starting the blog, she has published two books. A memoir style narrative called 'Finding My Way' and most recently, a poetry chapbook called 'Diary of a Dizzy Peri,' which includes her poems and thoughts on midlife, menopause and mental health. Both of these have formed the subject matter of her author talks, radio and magazine interviews.

This is her first work of fiction, something she has wanted to achieve for many years. Drawing upon her personal experiences, watching a close relative coping with dementia, this story is a tribute to precious memories, truth and acceptance. Her primary motivation in creating it, is for readers to see the person beneath the illness and to hear the stories that they still have to tell.

Karen lives in Surrey with her husband, Stuart, and two grown-up children, Matthew and Zoe. Between her writing commitments, she spends her time walking their cockapoo, Gizmo, baking a variety of treats, taking to the stage with her drama buddies and supporting her family in making their own memories together. She continues to write and enjoys the connections this brings. Perhaps she'll manage to find her turret by the sea soon – dreams sometimes come true.

Follow her writing journey on her website – karenhonnor.com

Blenheim Palace, Oxfordshire – 2020

Other titles available via Amazon -

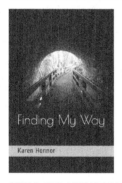

ISBN: 978-1070372862   *ISBN: 979-8643542551*